A STORY OF COMMUNAL HARMONY AND PATRIOTISM

SALUTE
the Souls

Dr. Kumar R. Bhushan

&

Arya Bhushan

www.chembila.com
info@chembila.com

www.chembila.com
info@chembila.com

Contents

Acknowledgments

In the continuous exploration of our musical expedition for the book project "YOUR SMILING FACE," we found ourselves tremendously moved by two compositions – one emphasizing communal harmony, and the other evoking a deep sense of patriotism. These musical compositions served as the catalysts that inspired us to craft a tale of communal harmony and patriotism. This is a perfect anecdote of the inner and outer struggles of humanity, both within the country and across its borders.

Diverging from conventional works of fiction, each principal character in this narrative embodies the essence of heroism and valor. Moreover, the ultimate sacrifice dwarfs even the tallness of the word 'hero.' Within the pages of this book, we set off on a pensive exploration of patriotism—an emotion that is incomparable.

We thank the music director, Mr. Rajesh Ghayal, the music programmers, and the talented singers who contributed to the composition of the songs. In particular, we are deeply indebted for the blessings and contributions of the legendary singers, namely, Mr. Kumar Sanu, Ms. Alka Yagnik, Mr. Udit Narayan, Ms. Sadhana Sargam, Ms. Anuradha Paudwal, Mr. Suresh Wadkar, Ms. Richa Sharma, and Mr. Amit Kumar, who have graced with their melodious voices to the songs within the book, now compiled and presented as "SALUTE the Souls."

We extend our gratitude to the numerous friends, critics, and well-wishers whose morale-boosting propelled us to shape the characters and scenes within the book.

Last but not least, we would like to express our gratitude to our editor, Mr. Nitin Dutta, for his professionalism and invaluable assistance throughout the entire publishing process.

"To our brave soldiers: Your courage lights the path to peace, your sacrifice echoes in our hearts. Thank you for standing strong and protecting us all. We salute you."

Genre: Conspiracy Thriller, Epic Saga, Musical, and Sentimental

USP: A story of communal harmony and patriotism

Logline: Salute the Souls - Intricately weaves communal unity and deep patriotism, delving into inner and outer struggles of humanity, both within the country and across its borders. Departing from conventions, heroes redefine sacrifice, embodying valor in a poignant embrace of incomparable patriotism that transcends boundaries, reshaping the essence of heroism.

Blurb: "Salute the Souls," magnificently weaves the threads of patriotism, love, sacrifice, duty, and revenge, forming a rich blend of heartstrings. Witness the stirring interplay of emotions, convictions, and actions that define the essence of who we are. From the resounding echoes of duty that ooze through generations to the animated melodies of sacrifice, each chapter unravels a compelling story of resilience, heroism, and the enduring power of love.

Music Album: SALUTE the Souls
Lyrics/Composition: Dr. Kumar R. Bhushan
Music: Rajesh Ghayal
Voice: Kumar Sanu, Alka Yagnik, Udit Narayan, Sadhana Sargam, Anuradha Paudwal, Suresh Wadkar, Richa Sharma, Amit Kumar, Khushboo Jain, Arvind Ojha, Nazim, Kewal Prajapati, Rakesh Singh

(The songs from this book are available on "CHEMBILA music" YouTube Channel, Facebook, Instagram, chembila.com, and major streaming platforms)

About the Authors

DR. BHUSHAN is adorned with academic degrees from institutions in both the United States and India. He has served in academic and scientific roles in various organizations within both countries. Throughout his academic journey, he has co-authored many peer-reviewed publications and presented lectures at various conferences. Additionally, Dr. Bhushan holds co-inventor status on several patents. Alongside his scientific pursuits, he has cultivated a passion for literature and is actively engaged in writing books and song lyrics.

ARYA BHUSHAN is an undergraduate student at Yale University, a prestigious Ivy League institution. He actively participates in various academic competitions and contests, showcasing his intellectual prowess. Arya's odyssey as a writer began in his formative years when he crafted an array of captivating short stories. His multidisciplinary education, combined with insightful discussions with his father, served as a wellspring of inspiration. Together with his father, he stepped aboard on a collaborative effort to pen their second book. With a quill dipped in the ink of passion, Arya aspires to create an extensive portfolio of both fiction and non-fiction works in the coming years, sharing his literary passion with the world.

Preface

In the sphere of human experience, certain themes weave through the fibers of our emotions, resonating with a depth that transcends time. These emotions, deep and timeless, reach into the very core of our humanity. Patriotism, love, sacrifice, duty, and revenge emerge as vivid strokes on the canvas of our lives, each imbued with a spectrum of feelings that stir the soul. "Salute the Souls" gently meanders through the rivulets of these emotions, setting forth on a poignant exploration of the interplay that shapes our persona.

Patriotism, a flame that ignites the spirit, draws forth sentiments that swell within the heart. The love for one's homeland, the fierce loyalty to a collective identity, and the poignant sacrifices made in the name of a nation form a symphony of emotions that resonate with every beat of the human heart. The pages unfold like a heartfelt anthem, evoking emotions that echo through the chambers of our shared memory.

Love, the universal language that transcends boundaries and challenges, is another guiding force in this narrative. It manifests in myriad forms — the love for family, for a partner, for comrades, and for one's homeland. These tales of love, whether enduring or fleeting, illuminate the complex depiction of human connections.

Sacrifice, a synonym for the resilience of the human spirit, emerges as a recurring keynote. Whether in service to a higher calling or for the sake of love, characters battle with the weight of sacrifice and find meaning under the shadow of terror. Throughout the recitals, we reflect on the intensive impact of selflessness and the enriched legacy it leaves behind.

Duty, an unyielding sense of responsibility, often becomes a driving force in the narratives presented here. Characters tussle with the demands of duty, be it to their nation, their family, or themselves. Duty becomes a crucible in which choices are forged, and destinies are shaped, prompting us to question our sense of responsibility in the grander scheme of life.

Revenge, a tempest of emotions, casts shadows, adding complexity to the narrative. Characters wage war with the visceral pull of vengeance, exploring the depths of anger, grief, and the blurred lines between justice and retribution. In these stories, emotions surge and collide, revealing the intricate dance of darkness within the human soul.

Each episode is a salutation to the human experience, reflecting the varied hues of our collective journey. Together, they form a mosaic that celebrates the resilience of the human spirit and the enduring qualities that define us as individuals and as a society. The entwining stories, elegant in emotion and complexity, form a topography of resilience, sacrifice, and the enduring spirit of humanity.

A bravery medal is a piece of metal woven into a thread. But when it gets carried as a legacy to generations, it becomes an accolade that any currency ever devised on this planet cannot buy. Therefore, let us extend our heartfelt salute to every warrior, be they clad in military uniform or everyday attire, individuals for whom the weight of their nation comes before even their own existence. Let us humbly bow in reverence to those souls for whom the foremost religion is humanity.

Dr. Kumar R. Bhushan & Arya Bhushan

Date: March 01, 2024

1. Introduction: Tejas' Wife & Son Visit Village

The road rested in quietness, observing the stillness of the predawn hours. It yearned for the sun to gently caress its surface with the warmth of morning light. A dense blanket of fog, like a mysterious guard, enveloped the pathway. It made the surroundings hazy, identical to rain droplets blurring even the finest megapixel camera designed by mankind. Nevertheless, the mighty sun, resembling a timeless artist, started painting the sky with its hues, gradually dissolving the fog's domination.

A rickshaw with a young 27-year-old lady and a 6-year-old child was the sole occupant of the road. As they approached a chowk (ring road), the young lady requested the rickshaw puller, "Brother…just here…here." She pointed to the left. "Please stop at the paving. Yes, here on the right side."

Confused and curious, the child asked, "Mom, were we not supposed to reach this place by midnight?"

The mother returned, "Yes, you are right, sweety. "I was worried that after getting down at the railway station, would we get a mode of transport at that hour of the night. However, the dense fog simmered the speed of the chugging train. So, a delay is not always bad. At times, it can be favorable."

The boy, least bothered about the merit or demerit of delay, asked, "But what is the purpose of our visit? Grandpa has departed from us. Can you tell me why we are getting down here?"

Ignoring the child, the young lady said to the rickshaw puller, "Brother take this…this," as she offered him ₹ 100.

The rickshaw puller replied humbly, "Madam, I do not have a change of hundred rupees' note."

"This is all yours."

"Madam, this is too much for the fare."

"This currency note weighs much less than the worry of transportation that had overpowered me. So, please keep it."

"Madamji, God bless you for this kind gesture. Goodbye." The rickshaw puller backtracked.

Screechingly, the child asked, "Mom, grandpa is not here. Where are we going?"

Hurriedly, the lady responded, "See this," as she grasped her son's hand and proceeded. Directing her finger straight ahead, she instructed the child, "Come here and take a look."

Before them stood a silver statue, larger than life, portraying a middle-aged man gazing at the horizon with a warm smile. Gradually, the duo tilted their heads upward as the lady explained to the child, "Look at him. This is your grandpa."

She held the boy's hands and guided him to clasp his palms together in a prayerful posture. Folding her hands, she taught the boy to pay respect to the statue. "Take blessing from him," she suggested.

Surprised and animated, the boy asked, "This is a statue. Why is grandpa a statue?"

The lady tried to hide her emotions behind her thick film of tears. However, she continued to pay her respects to the statue.

"Mom, why are you crying? I do not understand."

"No…no…I am not weeping," saying so, she tried to muffle her yowl.

Like the quizzical mind of a juvenile, the child still had inquiries for his mother, but she reassured him, saying, "I will answer all your questions. First, receive blessings from your grandfather. He will bestow love, wealth, wisdom, and more upon you. Now, let us proceed. I shall share everything with you."

The two made their way to the main road, where the traffic had started rolling. As they stood, waiting for the cars to pass so they could cross, a car suddenly came to a halt right in front of them. A voice hidden behind the backseat-tinted window emerged, addressing the young lady. "It is with God's grace, my child, Sanam, you have come here to visit us today!"

Holding the child's hand, the young lady stepped toward the backdoor of the motorcar. As the door swung open, a 75-year-old Christian man ornamented with a cross pendant necklace and three sets of prayer bead bracelets appeared. The lady promptly touched the old man's feet and instructed the child to follow the same by saying, "Touch the feet of another grandpa and take his blessing."

As the child touched his feet, the Christian man kissed the foreheads of both the mother and child, and he kindly invited them to take a seat in the car. He made space in the backseat to ensure they would all be comfortable. The man's name was John, an Englishman who arrived in India from Europe in his mid-20's as a tourist. Later, he became interested in exploring Indian culture after meeting an Indian girl whom he eventually married. During a severe flood, he visited the region to work on a TV documentary and was deeply inspired by a man known as "Masterji." John visited Masterji very frequently and finally, with his help, John settled down in his village.

John exclaimed, "Although it is late, I am very happy to see you here. It is great, my child, that at least you have come here."

After a brief pause, his tone sombered, "I understand that Tejas could not break his promise to Masterji. I also understand your reluctance to come back, despite the numerous efforts made by me and the villagers to persuade you to return earlier."

John took a moment to gaze out of the window, observing the passing trees and traffic with a somewhat distant interest. "My child, it is great that you guys are working hard to fulfill Masterji's dream."

Pointing at a nearby building, he continued, "With your help, we have modernized the school. My friend Masterji's soul ought to be getting a great deal of solace, and he may bestow his blessings upon us."

Moving his attention to the child, he placed his hand on the child's head and expressed, "My cutie baby, you are a true copy of Tejas. He was just like you, my dear. I still remember the day when your dad was about the same age as you, and Masterji used to send him to my house to learn English and French."

Upon their arrival at grandma's school, John was brimming with excitement when he spotted Laila, the anticipated visitor, at such an early hour of the morning. Laila had been tirelessly trying to get in touch with grandma for a long time, utilizing a military record contact associated with the late Tejas. Eventually, she managed to connect with John over the phone, who graciously provided her with instructions on how to visit grandma in the village. On the designated day of Laila's arrival, John arranged for one of his associates to pick her up from the nearby railway station.

John took the opportunity to introduce Laila to Sanam, who remained unaware of Laila's purpose. However, Laila very well knew that Sanam was Tejas' wife. In fact, upon Laila's return from Pakistan, she had been desperately searching for Sanam.

Following JK's instructions, Laila was determined to locate Sanam in Jammu and Kashmir (J&K). Laila hoped that by finding Sanam, she could establish a channel to reach grandma, who lived in another part of the country, and deliver the bravery medal that JK had bestowed upon her. Furthermore, JK had entrusted Laila with the responsibility of extending assistance to Sanam if the need arose. As an individual residing as an outsider in J&K, Sanam found herself in a distinct social and political context. In contrast, Laila, equipped with local influence and authority, was better positioned to provide the necessary support.

This medal served as a testament to JK's bravery, delivering a message to both grandma and Sanam. It was originally given by grandma to Tejas, who had handed it over to JK after a turn of events.

JK wished to return the medal to grandma through Laila as proof of eliminating the terrorist behind Tejas' death and the insult to India. Moreover, JK showcased his loyalty to his dear friend Tejas by giving up his life to defend his nation, assassinating the terrorists on Pakistani soil.

Regrettably, Sanam had relocated from J&K to Punjab, making it challenging for Laila to track her down. Finally, after persistent efforts, Laila managed to obtain Tejas' contact address from his military records. It was John who answered her call and provided her with detailed instructions on how to travel to the village and meet grandma, ensuring a successful reunion.

After a while, everyone grew desperate to see grandma, who was severely ill due to her old age. Sanam, the child, and Laila were accompanied by John as they entered grandma's room. There she lay on a ventilator, unable to speak much. Nevertheless, as the visitors approached, she greeted them all with a sigh of a smile and motioned for them to come closer. Grandma recognized Sanam and understood that the child was Sanam's son and her grandson Tejas, as he bore a striking resemblance to Tejas at that age. Filled with affection, she gestured to the three of them to come closer so she could hug them.

John informed grandma that Laila was on her way to visit her personally to deliver a message regarding Tejas' close friend, JK. Laila was anxious to recount to grandma JK's brick-walled loyalty and bravery in the name of friendship and the nation. John had heard all the stories directly from grandma and Masterji himself, as Masterji had confided them to John. With grandma listening intently, each of them began narrating their own stories, and she attentively absorbed every word.

The story leaped into a decades-long flashback

The platform started to vibrate, initially very subtly, but it gradually intensified into a mild tremor as the coal engine came to a gradual halt at the train station. A gentle wind complemented the soft squeak of the brake, a noise quickly drowned out by the 4 AM station bell. Thick fog encapsulated the lonely platform on a dark December morning. Yet, it did not deter tea sellers from knocking and yelling through coach windows. "Hot and only hot tea. Guzzle and beat the cold!"

Inside the seventh window from the end, a young man in his twenties, hailing from the village, boasts a striking appearance that mirrored his innocence, good looks, and muscular physique. He was asleep, his head resting against the metal window grille. He woke up in an instant as the tea seller walked by. Taking stock of the surroundings, he buzzed to the tea hawker, "What station are we at?"

"Delhi," the tea seller quipped, and then continued to advertise his piping hot tea.

With a sense of urgency, the man exclaimed, "Oh my god I have to get down here!" Hurriedly, he grabbed his shawl, flung a Gandhi-like long-strap handbag on his shoulders, and ran toward the exit door. Suddenly, the train whistled for departure and slowly started snaking forward. Desperate not to miss his stop, the man struggled to step down from the moving train, which had now left the platform. As he was about to leapfrog over, he toppled from the last steps. Yet he remained unhurt as he rolled onto the thick vegetation near the track. Brushing the grass off his shirt, he stood up to start his trek back to the station. The low visibility impeding his sight, he struggled to brisk to the platform and find his way out of the station gate.

Just like the interior, the area outside the station appeared barren, with only a sparse flow of vehicles and the cacophony of morning birdsong. Handicapped beggars with cut hands or feet were the sole occupants of the roads at this hour, snoozing on the sidewalk.

The man grappled for a long time to find some conveyance to reach his city destination. Amid his quest, he suddenly caught the faint sound of a child's cry, intensifying with each passing second. He followed the noise to the far end, where half a dozen street dogs barked and attempted to jump atop the cubic-yard dumpster.

Doubting whether the noise originated from the trash can, he disregarded it and turned in the opposite direction to search for an auto-rickshaw, hoping to depart from the location. Nonetheless, the escalating cry of the child, amid the harsh barking of the dogs, captured the man's focus, prompting him to inch toward the trash. Faced with the challenge of driving the dogs away, he enticed them to leave by tossing the leftover food from his lunchbox. This diverted the dogs' attention to the distant tidbits.

The baby continued to wail as the man slowly attempted to look into the trash. To his utmost surprise, the man found a newly born baby tied in an infant car seat and partially covered in a blanket. As soon as the baby spotted him and their eyes met, the baby ceased crying and trying to sense him. The newborn extended his tiny finger toward the man's forehead, reaching out to make contact. Pity in his eyes, the man soberly locked eyes with the innocent baby. It seemed like the rising decibel of the bustle around had hushed for some time. The young man made an effort to amuse the baby, momentarily forgetting his origin, the purpose of his journey, his destination, and the people he was scheduled to meet in a few hours.

He attempted to lift the baby in his arms and cradle him, but then it dawned on him – the purpose of his journey, and the impending meeting with his girlfriend and her family. Fear overcame him, and he carefully put the baby back in the car seat, which lay inside the garbage bin. The man then attempted to discreetly exit the location. Yet, the intensifying crying of the baby simmered his steps down. Moreover, as the dogs drew near the cubic-yard trash container once more, he shifted his attention back to the baby. The concerned man raised the infant in his arms and shielded the little one beneath his shawl.

He realized the baby was hungry, so he tried to arrange some milk for him. This man's name was Masterji.

Masterji proceeded to walk along the sidewalk of the road toward a nearby shopping complex, where he noticed a lone open shop at dawn. Inside the shop, he purchased a baby's milk bottle. With the bottle in hand, he began feeding the hungry baby, alleviating the child's distress and allowing him to consume the nourishing milk.

Inquisitive about the availability of an auto-rickshaw for his journey to Lodhi Road, Masterji approached the shopkeeper and politely inquired, "Excuse me, can you please guide how I can board an auto-rickshaw for Lodhi Road?"

The shopkeeper cordially responded, "Sir, auto rickshaws are primarily available at the railway stations, although, at this early hour, it is unlikely to find one. Perhaps, as the day progresses and the sun rises further, approximately within the next hour, you may have a better chance of securing an auto rickshaw for your destination."

Masterji began walking along the sidewalk, heading toward the railway station. He carefully rested the baby in his arms, ensuring the child was protected by his shawl. The baby's face was exposed, and the little one was engrossed in drinking milk without any interruption.

Masterji walked toward the railway station, hopeful of finding an auto-rickshaw that would take him to his ultimate destination.

Rita Sirohi and her family members were traveling back from the airport in a motorcar, having just picked up her father. Initially, their plan was for Rita to introduce Masterji to her father at their residence, where Masterji had been invited for a marriage proposal. However, fate took a different turn when they unexpectedly encountered Masterji on a road near the railway station during their return journey.

As the motorcar drew near to Masterji, Rita's family members could not help but engage in conversation, observing someone walking with a baby in the early morning hours along a deserted road. As the car's headlights lit up Masterji, Rita promptly directed the driver to pull the brakes. Startled, the driver complied, coming to an abrupt stop. Rita's family members were taken aback by Rita's sudden order to stop. Their amazement only deepened when she instructed the driver to reverse the car and trail the man walking along the road.

Masterji, too, was taken aback by the sudden stop of the motorcar and became frightened as the vehicle began reversing toward him. In his bewildered state, he gathered that these individuals might have some connection to the baby he was holding. A blend of relief and timidity overcame him as he considered the possibility of passing on the baby to them and being relieved of the infant's care. He cautiously moved toward the reversing car but grew increasingly nervous and scared when he noticed Rita inside the vehicle.

Rita was also shell-shocked to see Masterji holding a newborn baby. Her family members shouted at her, demanding to know what was going on. Finally, in broken words, she said, "That's him—our guest for today."

From the very start, Rita's family, especially her father, had strongly opposed her selection of an ordinary middle-class individual like Masterji from a rural background. The majority of the family members were in agreement with her father's perspective. Although they had agreed to meet Masterji, they were considering their options, hoping to find some excuse or weakness in him during their meeting. They intended for Rita to notice these flaws and subsequently distance herself from him. Brushing off the marriage proposal without a face-to-face meeting with Masterji would pose a challenge, as her father was well aware of his daughter's stubborn nature.

Coming across Masterji with the baby offered her father a chance to manufacture an excuse and raise questions about Masterji's reputation. Initially sensing and understanding the situation, he started playing the blame game and signified that Masterji might already be married or involved in an illicit relationship with another woman. Her father suggested that the baby was the outcome of the relationship between Masterji and the other woman. He went on to emphasize to Rita that Masterji and the baby's mother had a disagreement, which led the woman to entrust the baby to Masterji. That left him with the responsibility of caring for the child, despite it being against their wishes.

Amidst the tumultuous scene, Masterji made an effort to elucidate the facts, but Rita and her family members vehemently interrupted him, refusing to allow him to clear up the misconceptions. Instead, they resorted to physically confronting him. In a desperate attempt to protect the innocent baby, Masterji prioritized the child's safety over his own defense. In the heat of the moment, as Masterji attempted to shield the baby, he realized that the child had been struck. Rather than defending himself, he focused on safeguarding the defenseless infant.

Tragically, the situation took a turn for the worse when Rita, consumed by anger and disillusionment, slapped Masterji, accused him of lacking character, and demanded that he leave. Before departing, she expressed her hatred for him and declared that she never wanted to see his face again.

As Masterji left the scene, shattered dreams and a broken heart became his companions. The false accusations and rejection he endured marked a turning point in his life, propelling him on a journey of healing and self-discovery.

2. Upbringing of Tejas

At first, Masterji grappled with the dilemma of how to handle the baby and where to leave the child before heading back to his village. He had developed a deep emotional bond with the baby and found the idea of parting ways, whether by abandoning the child or sending it to an orphanage, too heart-wrenching to bear. Internally torn, he was uncertain about whether to leave or part with the baby, given the strong connection he had formed. Ultimately, he resolved to take the baby back to his village with him.

Arriving in the village with the baby late at night, Masterji was too afraid to face his grandma. Instead, he approached John, seeking support and explaining everything that had transpired in the city. John, understanding Masterji's courage and compassion toward the baby, despised the woman who had caused Masterji so much suffering during his journey. He accompanied Masterji to talk to grandma, acting as his advocate and explaining the circumstances and experiences Masterji had endured.

Grandma was taken aback to see Masterji returning from the city with a baby. She was curious to know what had happened to him and whose baby he had brought home. Masterji was unable to face his grandma directly, but with John's help, he managed to explain the situation to her. After John's explanation, grandma comprehended Masterji's predicament and Rita's betrayal.

Both John and grandma proposed the idea of Masterji taking the baby to an orphanage. Nevertheless, Masterji was overcome with sentimentality and resolved to keep and raise the baby as his own son. Initially, grandma, apprehensive about societal judgment and potential complications for Masterji's future marriage, hesitated to agree. However, as time passed, she too developed an affection for the baby. Enchanted by the baby's radiant face, she named him "Tejas," and decided to keep him at her home, raising him as Masterji's son.

Whenever grandma inquired about Masterji's marriage plans, he would always delay his response, citing his current responsibilities and his commitment to raising Tejas. However, he assured grandma that he would inform her when the time was opportune for marriage. Nevertheless, that appropriate time never seemed to come. In time, grandma stopped pressuring Masterji to marry, understanding that Rita's betrayal had left him emotionally scarred and wary of trusting another woman. She also recognized the burden of his work and his dedication to raising Tejas, understanding that Masterji was preoccupied and busy with his responsibilities.

Masterji had to face the harsh reality of societal resistance and boycott due to Tejas. The villagers harbored a belief that Masterji had been involved in an illicit relationship with a woman in the city, and Tejas was seen as the product of that relationship. The community's judgment and gossip weighed heavily on Masterji's shoulders. To shield Tejas and gain the villagers' acceptance, he took responsibility and stressed that the child was his own, regardless of the circumstances surrounding the baby's birth. However, the villagers took advantage of the situation and did not miss an opportunity to mock Masterji because of Tejas.

The societal backlash extended to grandma's school as well. The villagers, influenced by their misconceptions about Masterji's character, boycotted the school, believing that it was under the management of a man with a tarnished reputation. They feared that their children might be negatively influenced by Masterji's alleged immorality. The cut-off placed grandma's school in a precarious situation.

Despite the initial resistance, both Masterji and grandma remained resilient and committed to their principles. They continued to uphold their disciplined approach to life, gaining respect and admiration from those who knew them well. As time passed, their single-minded dedication and reputation began to influence the villagers' perception.

Gradually, the wounds started to heal, and the villagers began to reconsider their stance. They witnessed the genuine love and care Masterji and grandma provided to Tejas, recognizing that their actions spoke louder than any rumors or gossip. As their trust in Masterji's character and grandma's commitment to education was reestablished, the villagers gradually resumed sending their children to grandma's school.

The return of the villagers' children to the school marked a pivotal turn of the tide, signifying a fresh start where preconceived ideas and judgments were set aside. The bond between Masterji, grandma, and Tejas became a symbol of resilience and love, gradually eroding the prejudices that had once plagued their community. The village started to accept Masterji and Tejas as integral parts of their community, realizing that judgments based on misinformation could lead to unfair treatment.

From his earliest memories, Tejas endured a relentless onslaught of teasing and ridicule from both the children and some selected adults in the village. They branded him as an "illegal child," alleging that Masterji had brought him as a newborn baby from the city, with his mother's identity remaining a mystery. This stigmatizing label plagued Tejas wherever he went. The schoolchildren and villagers, influenced by superstitions, isolated him, believing he brought bad luck, and avoided any interaction with him. The hostility escalated at times, leading to groups of children physically assaulting Tejas, their aggression driven by his concealed maternal lineage.

When Tejas dared to stand up against his tormentors, they resorted to manhandling him and relentlessly pursued him to his doorstep, taunting him as an "illegal child." Tears streamed down Tejas' face as he sought solace in the comforting embrace of his grandmother or Masterji. Even Masterji could not evade their hostility, confronting allegations of moral misconduct, and grandma carried the weight of providing shelter to a man and his supposedly illegitimate child. The tormentors resorted to pelting stones at Masterji's home, an ongoing display of their dissatisfaction with the family. Such trying times tormented Masterji, Tejas, and grandma. It made their lives an ongoing battle against the village children's relentless teasing and hostile conduct.

During Tejas' formative years, he turned to Masterji, eagerly seeking answers to unravel the mystery of his parentage and to discover the identity of his mother. Masterji, understanding the suffering his son endured, consistently downplayed Tejas' questions, soothing him with a calm demeanor. He weaved a tale of a mother lost in the city during a fair visit, emphasizing that she would one day return to find him.

Masterji urged Tejas to disregard the rumors circulated by the villagers and the envy they held toward him. Rather, he referred to him as a child born into a prosperous and respected family. He instilled in Tejas an unflagging belief that these individuals would ultimately discover the truth and come forward to apologize for their misguided judgments. Tejas held onto Masterji's words, deriving comfort and fortitude from their discussions, paying no heed to the spiteful rumors that swirled around him.

Tejas's unyielding trust in Masterji's affirmations became his guiding light. Despite the trials he endured and the persistent mistreatment, he held onto the hope that one day the truth would prevail, and he would find acceptance and understanding within the village. The tireless love and support of Masterji, grandma, and their unbreakable familial bond allowed Tejas to find resilience in the face of adversity. Amid the ceaseless teasing of the village children and the hardships they brought, Tejas's steadfast belief in a promising future propelled him forward. That perception carried the weight of their collective dreams.

As Tejas entered his teenage years, he observed that Masterji would often become engrossed in reading certain letters when he was alone. Tejas noticed a tinge of solitude and sadness in Masterji whenever he looked at those letters. Later, when Tejas was in high school, he recollected those moments and decided to root out the truth. He secretly obtained and read Masterji's letters, discovering that Masterji had a girlfriend named Rita.

Tejas had grown up to be an active and sometimes mischievous young person. He occasionally played affectionate pranks on Masterji, pretending to be his stepson. Tejas also engaged in playful teasing with grandma. Most often he teased her by saying," Hey grand old lady from the last century!!"

The young lad decided to tease Masterji by mentioning the name of his girlfriend, Rita. He hired an elderly beggar woman near his school, paying her to make a prank call to Masterji, pretending to be Rita and expressing her love for him, and her desire to meet him in the city. Yet, Masterji had reservations about the voice on the phone since it lacked the distinctive Haryanvi Jat accent that Rita usually spoke in. In response, Masterji played a reverse high jink to tire out the woman on the other end of the line.

Tejas repeated these incidents multiple times, hiring different women to make clownery calls to Masterji. Although Tejas enjoyed these experiments, Masterji was not easily fooled by Tejas' tricks every time.

As Tejas continued his playful monkey tricks on Masterji, he found it increasingly challenging to catch him off guard. Masterji had developed a keen sense of awareness and could easily distinguish between genuine calls and prank calls. Nevertheless, Tejas persisted in his mischievous endeavors, always searching for new ways to tease and entertain Masterji.

One day, Tejas stumbled on an idea he believed would be a remarkable surprise for Masterji. He, with the help of his friends, masterminded an elaborate plan to make it seem like Masterji would receive a prestigious award for his educational contributions.

With the assistance of his friends, Tejas spread the news throughout the village. The rumor quickly spread like wildfire, capturing the attention and curiosity of everyone. The villagers, eager to witness this supposed honor bestowed upon Masterji, eagerly anticipated the day of the event.

On the designated day, the village gathered in a central location, buzzing with excitement and anticipation. Tejas had meticulously organized the entire spectacle, ensuring that every detail appeared legitimate. As the time approached, Masterji arrived, unaware of the gag that awaited him.

When Masterji entered the venue, he was met with thunderous applause and cheers from the villagers. It was an overwhelming sight for Masterji, who could not comprehend the reason behind such grand recognition. As he stood on the stage, Tejas emerged from the crowd, holding a microphone, ready to reveal the truth behind the tomfoolery.

Tejas spoke to the audience, recounting their playful pranks and how he had organized this detailed frolic as a heartfelt gesture of love and appreciation for Masterji. He expressed his admiration for

Masterji's dedication to education and his unwavering support as a father figure.

The villagers, initially thunderstruck by the revelation, soon found themselves caught up in the spirit of the moment. Laughter filled the air as they realized the extent to which Tejas had gone to pull off this horseplay. Masterji, though initially taken aback, could not help but join in the laughter, touched by the depth of Tejas' affection and the effort put into the mischievousness.

From that day forward, the relationship between Masterji, Tejas, and the villagers transformed. The once icy atmosphere thawed, replaced by a sense of camaraderie and shared laughter. Masterji, respected for his resilience and good humor, became an integral part of the village community, while Tejas was accepted by the other children, who now saw him in a new light.

As time went on, the memory of the prank faded into the background, but the bond between Masterji, Tejas, and the villagers continued to thrive. The incident served as a reminder of the power of laughter, forgiveness, and genuine connections that can bridge gaps and heal wounds.

Tejas learned valuable lessons about the impact of his actions, understanding that even mischievous pranks should be rooted in love and respect. Masterji, in response, cherished Tejas' playful spirit and recognized the momentousness of being blissful even during the troughs of life.

Masterji and Tejas continued their village journey as an inseparable team, now feeling a deeper sense of belonging and acceptance from a once-resistant community. Getting eyeball-to-eyeball with new challenges and adventures, their bond grew stronger, fueled by the laughter and love that had evolved their lives.

Masterji and Tejas became an inspiration to others in the village. Their ability to overcome societal resistance and transform negativity into laughter and unity left a lasting impact on the community.

With their newfound popularity, Masterji and Tejas took the opportunity to address the deep-rooted prejudices and misconceptions that had plagued their lives. They organized awareness campaigns and community discussions to promote understanding and empathy among the villagers. Engaging in candid conversations and sharing personal narratives inspired the community to question their preconceived ideas and adopt a more inclusive mindset.

Tejas, in particular, became a spokesperson for the rights and dignity of children who faced discrimination and bullying. His experiences as an "illegitimate" child fueled his passion to advocate for inclusivity and kindness. Tejas, alongside Masterji, started initiatives to support marginalized children, ensuring they had access to education, resources, and a safe environment to grow.

The village began to witness a gradual shift in mindset. People went from hating Tejas to admiring and respecting him for his strength and determination. Former bullies became his closest pals, learning about empathy and the consequences of their actions.

Once worried about the social consequences of raising Tejas, grandma observed the pronounced influence of love and acceptance. She became an ardent supporter of Masterji and Tejas, actively participating in their community efforts and providing unfaltering support.

As the years passed, Tejas grew into a confident and compassionate young adult. The scars of childhood teasing and prejudice faded, replaced by a deep-rooted sense of self-worth and a commitment to creating a better world. Inspired by Masterji and his own experiences, Tejas dedicated his career to social work, aiming to break down societal barriers and promote equal opportunities.

Masterji, too, found solace and fulfillment in the positive impact he had made on the lives of others. The once-isolated headmaster became a beloved figure in the village, admired for his compassion, wisdom, and steadfast dedication to education. His commitment to shaping young minds and encouraging a nurturing environment in grandma's school became a beacon of hope for generations to come.

3. Village: The Tussle between the Local Communities

Grandma's school and John's house were in proximity, separated only by a road that led in two distinct directions. One path led to a Hindu village, while the other led to a nearby Muslim village. This road was a lifeline connecting the two communities, yet it also served as a catalyst for tension and communal discord.

On the path from the school to the Muslim village, there was a roundabout named "Chowk" with a small market and local shops. Two mini-roads diverged from Chowk, each heading to different small villages. The Hindu village lay closer to the school compared to the Muslim village. The distance between these two settlements was just under a mile. The Hindu village was entirely Hindu, whereas the Muslim village had about 90% Muslims and 10% Hindus, with a population around two-thirds that of the Hindu village.

While the Muslim community had its own religious school, called Madrasa, some liberal Muslims preferred to send their children to grandma's school. Here, Hindu and Muslim children shared the same space, learned together, and studied side by side. Despite the majority of villages in the sub-district being Hindu-populated, there was a significant Muslim population as well. Some Muslim villages even surpassed the average Hindu-populated village in size.

The vicinity of Masterji's Hindu village and the neighboring Muslim village led to a volatile environment of communal unrest. A single road traversed both communities, passing through the Hindu village toward the town and the expansive Muslim village, home to the revered Akbar mosque. Similarly, the road originating from the Hindu village extended through the Muslim village, ultimately reaching another town where a magnificent temple devoted to Goddess Durga was located. In the Hindu village, near grandma's school, a small temple dedicated to Lord Ram and Lord Shiva adorned the roadside. Likewise, the Muslim village had a modest mosque situated by the side of the road.

The presence of these religious sites along the shared roadways often fanned the flames of communal tension and rivalry. The communities often argued over sharing religious spaces, such as temples and mosques. Typically, Hindu villagers protested the intrusive Azan loudspeaker broadcasts, especially the early morning and late-night calls. These broadcasts, emanating from both the Muslim village and mosques across the region, were deemed disruptive, upsetting the villagers' peace. The Hindu villagers were also concerned about occasional loudspeaker broadcasts of Muslim religious preaching and cultural festivals.

Conversely, Muslims lamented the loud and overpowering broadcasts of religious ceremonies such as Aarti from the Hindu temples. They also considered the routine religious sermons, music, and cultural festival broadcasts to be objectionable. The communities often engaged in quarrels and conflicts, sometimes over apparent reasons and at other times seemingly for no reason at all, provoking the entire community.

One of the most hot-button flashpoints between the Hindu and Muslim communities was the religious processions that traversed the shared road. Communal disturbances and clashes frequently arose during religious processions. The road linking the Hindu and Muslim villages symbolized this division, as each community asserted its religious and cultural practices along its course. Both communities held fervent religious beliefs and were deeply invested in their respective processions, considering them sacred and of utmost importance.

The Hindu villagers paraded from their village temple to the grand temple of Goddess Durga in the nearby town. These processions were characterized by lively music, colorful decorations, and devotees expressing their faith through dance and prayer. The sound of drums and cymbals filled the air as the procession made its way through the village, accompanied by chants and hymns.

Similarly, the Muslim community held processions from their mosque to the renowned Akbar mosque located in the vast Muslim village. The rhythmic recitation of religious verses, passionate sermons, and displays of devotion marked these rituals. The participants marched together, united in their faith, as the sound of prayers and religious songs echoed through the village.

As fate would have it, these religious rallies intersected at crucial points along the shared road. The Hindu ceremonies would pass near the mosque in the Muslim village, while the Muslim procession neared the small temple in the Hindu village. These intersecting points and moments often became catalysts for communal discords.

Tempers would flare and clashes would erupt as emotions ran high during these encounters. Troublemakers from both communities took advantage of the situation. They would pelt stones, chant provocative slogans, and try to incite violence in the crowd. These spurs escalated peaceful religious observance into chaotic conflicts, frequently leading to minor riots.

The Muslim population in the region had been converted from Hinduism during the rule of past Muslim rulers, further dividing the society. Scores of ongoing issues and rivalries between Hindus and Muslims persisted, stemming from their conflicting beliefs and traditions. For instance, Hindus regarded cows as sacred animals and worshiped them, forbidding their slaughter. Conversely, Muslims did not share this prohibition. These differences in faith led to countless disagreements and challenges between the two communities, which seemed unlikely to be resolved anytime soon. Moreover, disparities in infrastructure, resources, and socioeconomic opportunities between Hindu and Muslim villages amplified existing tensions.

Considering the delicate situation, the local administration and peace-loving individuals remained vigilant during these occasions. However, sporadic ruckus would still erupt, occasionally spreading beyond the village boundaries into neighboring regions. Both sides resorted to irksome slogans and actions to incite violence. The use of derogatory and inflammatory language, as well as stone-throwing, would often trigger riots. While some villagers treated these incidents as commonplace, others yearned to leave the village during religious festivals or even permanently, seeking a more peaceful abode elsewhere.

At times, the Muslim village received support from neighboring Muslim communities, exacerbating the complexity of the situation.

Nonetheless, the outnumbered Muslim community faced a backlash from the larger Hindu population in the vicinity, causing a brief displacement of Muslims from the region for several days.

In the midst of this communal turmoil, two individuals stood out as beacons of hope and advocates for peace. Masterji and John, both highly educated and respected in their communities, played a key role in trying to bridge the divide between the Hindu and Muslim villagers.

Masterji, known for his wisdom and impartiality, commanded respect from both communities. Despite allegations of partiality from both parties, he remained resolute. Masterji was committed to promoting understanding and harmony among Hindus and Muslims. His broad-mindedness and unfluctuating commitment to equality earned him the trust and admiration of many.

John, on the other hand, was an outsider who had come to the region with a genuine desire to contribute to its development. Although he did not share the same religious background as the villagers, he was well-versed in their traditions and customs. John's impartiality and empathy allowed him to build bridges of understanding between the two communities.

Both Masterji and John recognized the need for dialogue and transparent communication to dispel misconceptions and bolster empathy. They organized community gatherings, where members of both communities could come together and share their perspectives, fears, and aspirations. These forums created a safe space for individuals from both communities to voice concerns, grievances, and seek common ground.

Masterji and John also organized interfaith events and cultural exchanges, where Hindu and Muslim villagers could experience each other's traditions and customs firsthand. These conventions showcased the rich diversity within the region and underlined the shared values and aspirations of both communities.

Their efforts were not without challenges. There were times when their impartiality was questioned, and they faced criticism from those who believed they were compromising their own faiths. Muslims would accuse Masterji of bias toward Hindus, given his Hindu background. Whereas, some Hindus alleged that Masterji had converted to Islam, hence his advocacy for the Muslim community. Nevertheless, Masterji remained broad-minded and impervious to these allegations.

Amidst the struggles, glimmers of hope persisted. There were instances of Hindu and Muslim villagers coming together during times of crisis, setting aside their differences to support one another. These acts of unity and solidarity provided a ray of hope, a reminder that peaceful coexistence was not an impossible dream.

The road between grandma's school and John's house, although physically separating the Hindu and Muslim villages, also held the potential to serve as a bridge. It could be a symbol of connection, a pathway toward understanding and acceptance.

Over time, the combined efforts of the administration, community leaders, educators, and peace-loving individuals began to yield positive results. The instances of communal clashes became less frequent.

Despite enduring challenges, the strides taken in promoting coexistence filled the hearts of the Hindu and Muslim communities with hope and optimism. They had come a long way from the days of bitter rivalry and violence. The journey toward lasting peace was not yet complete, but the path was clearer than ever before.

4. Tejas's Identity and College Life

Tejas went to Delhi for his higher studies at the prestigious Kirori Mal College. The bustling city offered him a world of opportunities and possibilities, and he was excited to embark on this new chapter of his life. As he settled into the boys' hostel, he could not help but feel a mix of nervousness and anticipation.

His first few days at college were a whirlwind of orientations, introductions, and getting to know his fellow students. But amidst the chaos, Tejas could not shake off his lifelong passion for the Indian military services. Ever since he was a child, he had been captivated by stories of bravery, honor, and patriotism. His father, Masterji, a wise and respected teacher, had instilled in him a deep sense of admiration for the armed forces. Whereas his grandma had regaled him with tales of their family's history of serving the nation.

Tejas's zest for the military continued to intensify as he advanced through middle school and high school. He enthusiastically engaged in the school's Bharat Scouts and Guides initiatives, refining his leadership abilities and nurturing a strong sense of camaraderie. Tejas frequently caught himself lost in daydreams, picturing himself proudly wearing the uniform and dedicating himself to the service of his beloved nation.

In college, Tejas became an integral part of a special initiative focused on motivating and training students who aspired to join the Indian army. It was a program that aimed at equipping young minds with the necessary skills, knowledge, and discipline required for a successful military career. Tejas cherished his role as a leading member of the program, organizing training sessions, conducting workshops, and inspiring his peers to pursue their dreams fearlessly.

A swayful moment in Tejas's life transpired during his college's annual day celebration. The distinguished guest for the event was none other than Rita, a prominent media magnate. Her very presence demanded the spotlight, and her words left a lasting impression on the youthful audience.

With eloquence and passion, she delivered a speech that not only captivated the students but also touched their hearts. Rita's inspirational address drew from her own life experiences, aiming to ignite the aspirations of the young minds in the hall. She shared a powerful anecdote about an individual with humble village origins who had been her college classmate. While she did not reveal the person's identity, she painted a vivid picture of this remarkable individual's journey and achievements. Her narrative resonated deeply with Tejas and his fellow students, leaving them motivated to pursue their dreams.

According to Rita, this person had initially enrolled in language classes but had a natural talent for information technology. Alongside his regular college courses, he followed his passion by attending additional training at another institute. His unwavering dedication led him to become one of the world's best software developers. Rita encouraged the new generation to follow their passions rather than being swayed solely by societal expectations or the pursuit of financial security.

Tejas could not believe his ears. With theatrical expressions and raised eyebrows, he looked at Rita without batting an eyelid, Tejas was stunned by the link between Rita's speech and Masterji's academic pursuits at Jawaharlal Nehru University (JNU). Masterji had recounted to Tejas his enthusiasm for software-related studies and his volunteer work at the Indian Institute of Technology (IIT) in a professor's lab. With a pronounced wave of goosebumps, it was like long-dead moments coming to life. It became evident to him that Rita was the same person who had attended JNU during the same period as Masterji. This revelation triggered memories of the sentimental love letter Rita had addressed to Masterji, which Tejas had come across.

Witnessing the past unfolding, Tejas became convinced that Rita might be his mother. Masterji had previously mentioned that Tejas's mother had been lost at a fair in the city and had brought him to the village. Tejas connected the dots and concluded that Masterji had concealed the truth about his mother. Driven by the desire to unravel the story of his origins, Tejas made up his mind to meet Rita and confront her about his identity and her connection to Masterji.

However, drawing up to Rita was nothing less than escaping an array of battalions. She was no ordinary person to approach. Rita was a celebrity conglomerate personality and the head of a major media business in the country. An entourage of guards and office staff who were skeptical of anyone attempting to get close to her walled her. Rita was married to another business tycoon and had a complete family with children.

Undeterred, Tejas persisted in his efforts to secure an appointment with Rita. He made countless phone calls, sent numerous emails, and even tried to reach out to her through various connections. Each time, he was met with rejection, threats, or dismissal. But Tejas refused to give up. He knew that to uncover the truth about his identity and her connection to Masterji, he had to confront Rita face-to-face.

When Tejas returned to the village during his break from college, he felt a sense of urgency to unveil the truth about his origins. He knew that directly questioning Masterji about Rita and his connection to her might not yield the answers he sought, as Masterji had guarded this secret for years. Further, questioning grandma would be futile. Therefore, Tejas chose to initiate a quest to gather information from external sources before confronting Masterji.

With a determined spirit, Tejas began his discreet investigation. He reached out to acquaintances, friends, and even distant relatives who might know Masterji's past. Through careful conversations and persistent inquiries, he managed to piece together fragments of information about Masterji's time at JNU, where he pursued higher studies.

Tejas learned about Masterji's commitment to software-related studies and his voluntary training with a renowned IIT professor. These details resonated with the stories Masterji had shared with Tejas during their conversations. The pieces of the puzzle began to align, strengthening Tejas's conviction that Rita and Masterji were indeed connected.

Before leaving the village to return to college, Tejas made a bold and calculated move. He secretly obtained a copy of the love letter that Rita had written to Masterji, expressing her deep affection and the promise of marriage between them. Holding this precious document in his hands, Tejas made a silent vow to himself that he would uncover the truth and bring clarity to his identity.

Though unsure of the consequences that awaited him, Tejas also felt a glimmer of hope. He believed that the love letter held the key to unlocking the hidden truths surrounding his birth and his connection to both Masterji and Rita. With the photocopy safely tucked away, Tejas geared up for the next phase of his adventure, knowing that the answers he sought lay in the meeting with Rita herself.

In a fearless, desperate bid for answers, Tejas strategically used Rita's love letter to Masterji to contact her. He formulated a plan, a carefully crafted narrative that would bring him face-to-face with Rita and force her to confront the truth he sought.

Tejas crafted a story, a claim that he was Rita's son, born as a result of her love affair with someone prior to her current married life. It was a daring move, one that carried both risk and potential reward. He knew that by threatening to expose the love affair letter to the media, he could tarnish Rita's reputation and disrupt her carefully constructed life. It was a drastic step, but Tejas believed it was necessary to know the truth about his own identity.

With resolute determination, Tejas dared the office personnel surrounding Rita to arrange a private and in-person appointment with her. He firmly stated that he would reveal the love letter's contents, exposing himself as Rita's illegitimate child if they did not comply. The shockwave of his claim reverberated through the entire office, leaving everyone thunderstruck and uncertain of how to proceed.

The magnitude of Tejas' threat and the potential consequences of his actions forced Rita's office personnel to act swiftly. Recognizing the seriousness of the situation, they immediately arranged for a confidential meeting between Tejas and Rita. Tejas, accompanied by an escort, was led to Rita's inner chamber, where the truth he longed for would finally come to light.

As Tejas wormed into the room, the escort trooped out of the room after gently shutting the door. His steps froze as he noticed Rita glaring at the canopy of trees from the wide window pane. Tejas cleared his throat, announcing his arrival. Taking a deep breath, Rita turned around. The edgy Rita moments before, now masked into a confident Rita, matching her stature. As Tejas stood before Rita, the layers of air gasped in anticipation and apprehension. Bearing the weight of his story and the love letter, Tejas knew that the meeting's outcome would determine his future and offer the answers he desperately sought. The room seemed to hold its breath as Tejas and Rita prepared to engage in a conversation that would unravel the mysteries of their intertwined past.

"Yes, young man, you have been holding my and my family's peace for ransom. Show me what you have got. But let me warn you, if this turns out to be a stunt to defame me, you shall be liable for penalties you will remember for life," Rita cautioned in a steely voice. Gulping a lump lodged in his throat, Tejas drew his hand to his shirt's pocket. He wordlessly handed over a page to Rita with an army of questions hovering on his mind.

As Rita's eyes fell upon the love letter addressed to Masterji and her marriage proposal, a flood of memories washed over her. She felt a mix of recognition and surprise as Tejas reiterated his claim that Masterji might have brought him to the village from the city, presenting himself as Masterji's son. However, Tejas's revelation that he was the result of a love affair between Rita and Masterji caught her completely off guard. It was as if the ghosts of the past, which had remained dormant for decades, suddenly awakened, reopening old chapters in her life.

Vivid images projected in Rita's mind, transporting her back in time. She could clearly recall that fateful day when she and her family had encountered Masterji near the city's railway station, carrying a newborn baby in his arms. On that very day, Masterji was to visit her father and family to discuss a marriage proposal she had conveyed in the same letter Tejas now handed to her.

The pieces of the puzzle were slowly coming together, and Rita could not help but feel a mix of confusion, disbelief, and a tinge of sadness. The realization that Tejas might indeed be the child she had unwittingly brought into the world struck her deeply. She could not deny the affection Masterji had shown toward the baby on that momentous day. She realized that Masterji had raised the child as his own, stepping into the role of a father, even though the circumstances of the baby's arrival remained a mystery.

As the weight of the past settled upon her shoulders, Rita struggled to process the complex emotions coursing through her veins. She knew that the truth behind Tejas's parentage lay within the depths of Masterji's knowledge. It was only he who could shed light on the origins of the child she had inadvertently become connected to. With a jumble of trepidation and a newfound determination, Rita urged Tejas to seek the answers he longed for from Masterji himself.

In that moment, Tejas realized that the truth he sought was within reach, yet he still had to navigate the complexities that lay ahead. The connection between Masterji, Rita, and himself had taken an unexpected turn, intertwining their lives in ways they had never anticipated.

Rita revealed the complete narrative to Tejas, delving into the story of how Masterji had been carrying a baby on that unfortunate day. However, she confessed that she did not know the baby's mother or any details about his origins. Yet, as she reflected upon their last encounter with Masterji, she strongly sensed that the same baby they were discussing was the one he had cared for so tenderly. Rita firmly believed that Masterji's attachment to the child indicated that he considered the baby to be his own son. Thus, she concluded that Masterji was indeed the baby's father.

Amidst the conversation, Rita emphasized her love for Masterji, but vehemently denied any suggestion of an illicit relationship between them. She expressed her disapproval of Tejas's claim that he was her child, firmly refuting the notion. Rita stood by her conviction that there had been no impropriety in her relationship with Masterji and that Tejas's assertion was unfounded.

As Rita uttered these words, her voice carried a compound of emotions, confusion, concern, and a hint of sorrow. She struggled to make sense of the past and reconcile the truth with the mysteries that still lingered. Deep within, she longed to provide Tejas with the answers he sought, but the truth eluded her grasp.

In that moment, Tejas found himself at a crossroads, torn between the words of a woman he believed to be his mother and the persistent questions that haunted his mind. He understood that the only way to unravel the enigma of his identity was to confront Masterji directly. Rita urged him to seek the truth from the man who had raised him, emphasizing that Masterji held the key to untangle the secrets of his past.

Tejas was left reeling in shock, tussling with the revelation that Rita denied being his mother. Confusion and a deep sense of loss consumed him as he tried to make sense of his true origins. If not Rita, then who could possibly be his mother? The question echoed relentlessly in his mind, fueling a burning desire for answers.

In the midst of this emotional turmoil, Rita firmly advised Tejas to seek the truth from Masterji himself. She stressed that only Masterji held the key to unraveling the mystery surrounding Tejas's birth and the circumstances that led to his arrival in their lives. Although she could not provide the answers he sought, Rita's staunch belief in Masterji's knowledge of the truth urged Tejas to direct his inquiries toward him.

Realizing the gravity of his accusations and their emotional toll on Rita, Tejas found the humility to apologize for his impulsive conduct and inappropriate approach. Acknowledging the distress he had caused, he asked for Rita's forgiveness, recognizing the insensitivity and audacity of his claims. Rita, displaying remarkable understanding and empathy, accepted his apologies, aware that his pursuit of the truth had triggered him to act hastily.

In her wisdom, Rita grasped the complexity of Tejas's emotional state and the overwhelming desire to uncover his identity. With genuine regard for both Tejas and Masterji, she bid him farewell, offering her support in his quest for answers. Rita understood the weight of the journey Tejas was about to undertake and the criticality of his search for self-discovery.

As Tejas departed, a blend of emotions surged through him—uncertainty, resolve, and a lasting appreciation for Rita's empathy. He stepped aboard on a new chapter in his life, armed with the knowledge that only Masterji held the truth he sought.

The path ahead was fraught with challenges and uncertainties, but Tejas had newfound clarity. With each step, he would inch closer to unraveling the tangled threads of his existence and finding the answers that lay buried within the enigmatic depths of his past.

Tejas's heart was heavy with the weight of the unknown, but he resolved to confront Masterji and demand the truth. With a renewed sense of purpose, he set out on a pathway that would redefine his understanding of himself and those he held dear.

As he walked away from Rita's presence, he carried with him a deep sense of appreciation for her honesty and guidance. Tejas's crusade for truth had just begun, but he knew that with perseverance and an undeviating spirit, he would eventually scoop out the secrets that lay hidden in the shadows of his past.

Tejas pondered deeply, his mind caught between his yearning for the truth and his concern for Masterji's feelings. He refrained from directly asking Masterji about his relationship with Rita or informing him that he had already met her. Tejas worried that such a straightforward approach might offend Masterji or jeopardize their bond.

In Tejas's heart, he held great respect for Masterji, a man who embodied integrity and kindness. He found it hard to believe that someone as noble as Masterji would engage in an illicit relationship, as alleged by Rita. He believed that Masterji had treated him with utmost care and affection, like a father would treat his child.

Yet, despite these thoughts, the lingering doubts continued to gnaw at Tejas's mind. The unresolved issue of his origin and identity tormented him, growing more complex with each passing day. He longed for the truth, a concrete understanding of who he truly was.

Desperation and disturbance propelled Tejas's determination to nose out the truth. He could not shake the feeling that his journey to self-discovery required knowing the full story, including the details of his connection to Rita. The uncertainty and lack of closure haunted him, urging him to take further steps in his excursion for answers.

Tejas decided to seek guidance from those who might have known more about Masterji and Rita's relationship. He reached out to old acquaintances and friends who were close to Masterji during his days at JNU. In discreet conversations, he carefully broached the subject, hoping to glean any additional information that could shed light on his existence.

However, the accounts Tejas gathered were fragmented and inconclusive. Some shared vague memories of Masterji and Rita's bond, mentioning their closeness but offering no concrete evidence. Others were unaware of any romantic involvement between them, leaving Tejas even more perplexed.

The entanglement deepened as Tejas discovered conflicting narratives and hidden layers within Masterji's past. He stumbled upon a diary belonging to Masterji, which contained cryptic passages hinting at an internal struggle and a forbidden love. Tejas poured over the faded pages, attempting to decipher the true meaning behind the words.

As Tejas delved deeper into his investigation, he also sought solace and perspective from those who had known Masterji for many years. The villagers, who deeply admired Masterji, recounted his selflessness, never-failing commitment to their welfare, and his role as a community mentor.

Yet, even within these accounts, Tejas found no concrete confirmation or denial of his connection to Rita. The villagers spoke of Masterji's love and care for him, but the specifics of his relationship with Rita remained elusive.

Tejas's desperation surged as he felt trapped in a web of unanswered questions. The truth seemed just out of reach, leaving him in a state of limbo. Despite his inner turmoil, he remained cautious and considerate, not wanting to disrupt the harmony and trust he shared with Masterji.

However, the weight of uncertainty became unbearable for Tejas. He yearned for closure, for the truth that would finally set him free from the shackles of doubt. With a heavy heart, Tejas made the difficult decision to confront Masterji directly, understanding that he needed to navigate the conversation with utmost sensitivity and respect.

Tejas mustered up the courage to initiate a dialogue with Masterji, aware of the delicate nature of the subject. He wanted to address his concerns about his identity and his connection to Rita, while also ensuring that he did not hurt Masterji's feelings or shatter the trust they had built over the years.

After the completion of the college break, the time came for Tejas to bid farewell to the village once again and return to his college. Masterji, filled with an alloy of sadness and pride, accompanied Tejas to the nearby village railway station. The platform, usually bustling with activity, now stood desolate, mirroring the heaviness in their hearts.

Tejas and Masterji stood there, their conversations filled with a meld of anticipation and unspoken concerns. The weight of Tejas' unanswered questions still burdening his heart, a surge of determination coursed through him. It was at this moment, amidst the silence of the station, Tejas found the courage to put Masterji to the ultimate test. In a moment of impulsive bravery, he reached out and gently placed Masterji's right palm on his head, his eyes locked with his father's.

"Baba," Tejas began, his voice trembling with a blend of desperation and determination, "I need to know the truth. I need you to swear, right here and now, whether I am your biological son."

Tejas had unknowingly placed Masterji in the midst of the most difficult test of his life. The weight of his love for Tejas, coupled with the knowledge of the truth he had carried for so long, made it unbearable for Masterji to face him. He was torn between protecting Tejas from the painful reality and honoring the unbreakable bond they shared.

Unable to look into Tejas's eyes, Masterji found solace in the palm resting on his head, silently praying for guidance and strength. Tears welled up in Masterji's eyes as he softly spoke, his voice ferrying the weight of a lifetime's worth of love and devotion. "Tejas, my son," he said, his voice quivering with emotion, "I cannot bring myself to swear on your head because the truth is more complex than a simple affirmation. You hold a special place in my heart, and I have loved and cared for you as my own, regardless of biology."

His heart ached at the thought of hurting Tejas, but he knew that finally, the time had come to reveal the truth, to unveil the intricate tapestry of their intertwined lives. In a voice filled with a blend of sorrow and affection, Masterji started to disclose the true account of Tejas's birth. He detailed the circumstances in which he found him as a newborn baby. Masterji shared the heart-wrenching tale of how someone had left him behind, the overwhelming emotions he had experienced, and the decision he had made to bring Tejas into his life.

As Masterji spoke, the pieces of the puzzle fell into place. Tejas listened intently, his heart heavy with regret and empathy. The story Masterji narrated was not one of deceit or manipulation, but of sacrifice and unconditional love. And as Masterji's words echoed in his ears, Tejas could not help but believe in the authenticity of his father's narrative.

Strengthening Tejas's resolve, Masterji disclosed the specifics of his last meeting with Rita. He confirmed aspects of her story and her accusations. Tejas realized that Rita's perspective, although distorted by her own pain, had held some truth. Yet, despite the revelations, Tejas's faith in Masterji remained set in stone.

A penetrating sense of regret washed over Tejas as he comprehended the sacrifices Masterji had made for him. He could not help but blame himself for the love that Masterji had foregone and the life he had chosen to dedicate solely to Tejas. The weight of that realization settled heavily on his shoulders.

Moreover, Tejas considered the thought that perhaps he was a harbinger of bad omens for Masterji. He was an unlucky presence that had prevented Masterji from pursuing his desires, including marriage and companionship. Guilt hula-hooped on Tejas mind, mingling with gratitude for the love he had received. His heart was chock full with the realization of Masterji's sacrifices.

On seeing Tejas immersed in deep negative emotions, Masterji reached out to him, offering comfort and reassurance. He spoke softly, his voice filled with genuine affection and gratitude, "Tejas, I consider myself incredibly fortunate to have found you. My son, because of you, I was saved from falling into the trap of Rita's deceitful love."

Masterji's eyes reflected a mixture of relief and vulnerability as he continued, "During that difficult time, I was not trusted or given a chance to explain myself. That experience taught me that true love is not just about passion and desire; it is about sacrifice and true-blue trust."

Tejas listened attentively, his demeanor calm and respectful. As an obedient student, he absorbed Masterji's words, realizing the magnitude of the lessons he was imparting. Masterji spoke with a composed voice, his gratitude evident, "I am grateful that I learned this valuable lesson at a young age. It safeguarded me from the potential disaster at a later age of trusting someone unfaithful and untrustworthy. Now, I have no worries because you are my lighthouse of hope in life. I thank God for saving me from an evil and deceitful woman."

As Tejas's train pulled to the platform, he readied himself to get on board. Nevertheless, Masterji continued to share his wisdom, delving into the complexities of human nature. He shared illustrations of both virtuous and shadowy aspects. Tejas absorbed every word, his love, admiration, and respect for Masterji, multiplying with each passing moment.

Tejas could not contain his emotions any longer and addressed Masterji with affection, "Baba, you are my savior, and 1 consider myself incredibly fortunate to have you as my father." Their bond, forged through love, sacrifice, and shared experiences, grew even stronger.

Masterji, with a gentle smile, urged Tejas to let go of the past and focus on the present. "Son, let's leave behind these irrelevant things. You are already my beloved son." With those words, the train began to pick up momentum, ready to depart from the platform.

As Tejas looked back at Masterji, his heart overflowed with gratitude and love. The train lugged him away, but their connection remained unbroken, transcending distance and time. Tejas carried with him the invaluable lessons and unconditional love bestowed upon him by Masterji.

And as the train disappeared into the horizon, Tejas commenced the next chapter of his life. He was armed with the wisdom and resilience he had gained through his father's love, Masterji. He realized that the love and sacrifice Masterji had shown him were immeasurable. Tejas understood that blood relations were not the only measure of family. He had been blessed with a father who had chosen him, loved him, and guided him throughout his life. Tejas was grateful that his path had led him to Masterji, who had nurtured him, shaped his values, and instilled in him a deep sense of patriotism.

Upon returning to college, Tejas resumed his responsibilities with renewed vigor. The experience had deepened his appreciation for the bonds of love and family. He immersed himself in his studies and army training program. Tejas became an icon for his peers to pursue their aspirations and instilled discipline and purpose in them.

Years passed, and Tejas emerged as a promising leader, driven by the values enrooted in him by Masterji. He graduated from Kirori Mal College with flying colors and appeared for the Indian Army officer selection process. His determination and passion carried him through the grueling tests, making him one of the top candidates.

Tejas's dream had finally come true. He was commissioned as an officer in the Indian Army, ready to set forth on a journey of selfless service and valor. With every step he took in his uniform, he honored the love, sacrifice, and guidance of Masterji, who had shaped his destiny and shown him the true meaning of family.

5. Tejas's College Trip

Tejas went on a college trip to Darjeeling, coinciding with a group of girls from Miranda House College, who were also vacationing there. One day, a few girls decided to go horse riding together. Among them, Sanam stood out as innocent and beautiful. However, some local guys took advantage of their knowledge of a trained horse that followed its master's whistles. In the past, these guys had tricked girls into riding the trained horse, leading them to isolated areas where they would misbehave, molest, or engage in other harmful acts.

Unfortunately, Sanam was assigned to ride the trained horse. After a short distance on a rough path, the bad guys diverted the horse away from the rest of the group and took Sanam to a secluded and bushy area in the jungle. There, in proximity to a cluster of local boys, they dismounted her from the horse and initiated verbal abuse and harassment. When she resisted, they forcibly removed her clothes, handcuffed her behind her back, and placed tape over her mouth to silence her. The boys proceeded to molest her.

Tejas and his friends were walking uphill toward their hotel when suddenly Tejas felt the need to relieve himself. He decided to divert downhill and signaled to his friends that he would catch up with them after he finished attending to nature's call. As he sang a Bollywood song and attempted to unzip his pants to urinate, he sensed some movement behind the bushes downhill.

This caught the attention of the local boys. Despite his fear of wild animals, Tejas cautiously slid downhill to investigate the situation. Through the bushes, he caught a glimpse of a handcuffed girl. He could see the hands of four boys, but their faces remained hidden behind the thick foliage. The girl's mouth was sealed, and her clothes were torn in a manner that threatened her modesty.

The local boys registered Tejas's movements, but they could not see him. At one moment, Tejas made eye contact with the girl in distress. Her eyes appeared to be praying to him for her life, as if she believed that God had sent him as a messenger to rescue her.

The girl's beauty, innocence, and allure struck a deep chord within Tejas, and he felt a cryptic connection with her. After confirming the boys were oppressing the girl, he mimicked different voices to create the illusion of an approaching group. He shouted, "Who are these bastards abusing a girl?! Hold on, hold on! Lady, we are coming to save you, hold on, hold on!"

Upon hearing the commotion, the local boys quickly fled from sight and concealed themselves in the bushes. However, as they realized that only one person was approaching the girl, they regrouped and launched an attack on Tejas. However, Tejas managed to draw near to Sanam, although a thicket of bushes kept them apart, resulting in a brief moment of eye contact.

Suddenly, one of the boys hurled a stone that struck Tejas's leg. Reacting quickly, Tejas removed his Northface fleece and threw it to Sanam, providing her with a means to cover herself. Despite his attempt to speak, Tejas was forcefully struck by another boy, causing him to fall and roll to the other side.

But then, something extraordinary happened. When the third boy tried to attack Tejas, an immense surge of energy coursed through him. Tejas moved forward, engaging all four criminal boys in a fierce tussle. He fought valiantly, preventing any of them from approaching the girl and ensuring her safety.

A tumultuous fight erupted as the criminals drew out knives and local-made pistols. Tejas managed to overpower and defeat nearly all of them. However, the last remaining assailant had a pistol and fired it at Tejas. With quick reflexes, Tejas survived the bullet and retaliated, delivering a powerful blow that knocked down the criminal. Sensing they were no match to the brute force of Tejas, the offenders ran head over heels and dissolved into the woods.

Unfortunately, during this intense exchange, Tejas inadvertently slipped and fell into a trench on the hill. The events that transpired afterward remained unknown, as nobody witnessed or had knowledge of what happened to Tejas at that moment.

In the meantime, Sanam's friends arrived to find her. After they had managed to free Sanam from the restraints, they tried to look for Tejas, but to no avail. Sanam began to fear that he might have become disoriented and descended further downhill, with slim chances of survival. Despite the uncertainty, she continued to pray earnestly for Tejas's safety.

Sanam's friends, concerned for their safety, convinced her to leave the area and return to the hotel. Reluctantly, she accompanied them, but her prayers persisted. She held onto her steadfast faith, firmly believing that the messenger of God could not perish. Sanam remained confident that Tejas would survive, and one day, in the divine plan, God would reunite them, allowing her to see him standing before her once again.

Tejas's companions, who had gone back to the hotel, grew worried upon realizing his absence. Therefore, they promptly initiated a search. Even though the girls had already left the location, Tejas's friends stumbled upon his muffler. Sensing something uninvited had happened to Tejas, they started tracking his footprints downhill in search of him.

Splitting in different directions, his friends started combing the hillock. Everyone was awestruck when one of them screeched, "Guys, come here at once." As the search team gravitated to the source of the shriek, they found Tejas lying unconscious on the edge of the cliff. Fortunately, he had landed on the cushion of dry leaves, so there was no internal injury. But as he was trying to resist the fall, Tejas received some bruises on his hands and legs.

One of his friends, who was tugging a water bottle, sprinkled water on Tejas's face, bringing him back to his senses. As Tejas opened his eyes, he got up in an instant and jawed, "Where is that girl? She was in deep trouble. Those rascals were trying to rob her of her dignity." Assuming Tejas was in a state of shock, one of his friends smirked, "Tejas, I think, when you went for the pee, the mountain fairy or maybe a witch noticed you. Seeing a young man with a herculean built-up, she could not resist entrancing you. But I wonder, how have you received wounds in your hands? Injuring the knees is understandable, though." Everyone present burst into side-splitting laughter, including Tejas.

They swiftly brought him back to the hotel room and sought the assistance of a doctor, who provided the necessary care to Tejas. Remarkably, by the following day, Tejas had made a complete recovery and was in perfect health once again.

Sanam shared the turn of events with her friends, recounting Tejas's acts of generosity and bravery as her savior. However, one of her friends tended to doubt boys' intentions, suspecting that they would engage in such cheap tactics to gain attention from girls. This friend suggested that Tejas might have masterminded the entire situation by hiring goons to harass Sanam, to gain sympathy and impress her.

Somehow, Sanam became influenced by her friends' unanimous support for the perspective put forth by the doubting friend. This led to her being somewhat brainwashed, as she began to adopt the view that Tejas had intentionally planned the entire incident to impress and gain her attention. However, deep within her subconscious, doubts persisted, and she could not fully accept her friend's point of view.

Despite the confusion, Sanam continued to pray for Tejas's well-being. She also started wearing his fleece whenever she went outside, hoping that if Tejas saw her enwrapped in it, he would recognize her.

After a couple of days, Tejas and his team departed from Darjeeling on a bus. However, shortly after they began their journey, Tejas spotted Sanam at a traffic stop. She was sitting at a dhaba (roadside eating joint), happily enjoying the food with her friends, and she was wearing Tejas's fleece. Sanam's radiant smile and the sight of her enjoying herself completely captivated Tejas. At that moment, he forgot about everything else, stood up, and made his way toward the front gate of the bus, intending to get off. This unexpected action surprised his friends, who were taken aback by his sudden move.

Tejas grew increasingly restless and desperate to reach Sanam as soon as possible. He approached the bus driver and earnestly requested him to stop and open the gate. However, the driver calmly responded, "Hold on, I will stop when we are out of the red light traffic."

Suddenly, the traffic light turned green, and the bus driver had to resume driving. The bus picked up speed, making it impossible for Tejas to get off at that moment. His friends managed to restrain him and assured him that he could disembark at a suitable location when the driver deemed it safe to stop. As the bus continued its journey, it traveled another two miles. Finally, an opportunity arose, and Tejas seized it, getting off the bus and attempting to hitchhike his way to the dhaba.

After a while, a kind-hearted individual stopped their car and offered Tejas a ride to the dhaba. Grateful for the assistance, Tejas accepted and eagerly made his way to the eatery. However, upon reaching the place, he discovered that it was now empty, and all the girls had already departed. Feeling disappointed, he approached the dhaba owner and inquired about the group of people who had been there. The owner informed him that the girls had just left for a bus that had recently left.

Tejas sprinted in search of a motorbike ride that would pillion-ride him to follow the bus carrying the girl. However, a challenge arose when he reached a four-way road crossing just one mile down the road. The destination of the girl's bus remained unknown. Using his intuition and intelligence, Tejas made an educated guess and chose the road that led toward the main city, hoping it was the right direction.

Standing atop a hill, Tejas spotted a bus downhill, moving in the opposite direction, with several dupattas fluttering from the windows. The bus navigated the switchback hilly road, zig-zagging down the hill, occasionally approaching and then moving away from Tejas. Though he knew it was nearly impossible to catch up to the bus, he exerted every effort to reach it, determined to reunite with the girl.

Sanam's beauty had captivated Tejas to such an extent that he found himself falling in love with her. Even though he did not know her name, her background, or if he would ever cross paths with her again, he could not help but dream about her. The image of her innocent and vulnerable eyes peeking through the bushes and her radiant smile at the dhaba had deeply imprinted on his mind. By this time, the bus had driven to distant quarters, and Tejas settled on a roadside pavement, echoing his emotions to the valley.

Lost in his thoughts and emotions, Tejas began singing the song, "*Door Hoti Hui Paas Aati Hai...*," expressing his longing for Sanam and how she seemed to come closer even when she was distant. The melody resonated with his feelings for her, allowing him to immerse himself in the realm of his dreams.

DOOR HOTI HUI PAAS AATI HAI
(*Voice*: Mr. Kewal Prajapati)

*Door hoti hui paas aati hai
kisi ki muskaan hum ko lubhati hai
door hoti hui paas aati hai
kisi ki muskaan hum ko lubhati hai
jaise dil me kamal khil gaye ho
ho ho ho ho ho ho*

*Koi khushboo fizaon se aati hai
jo sanson ko mere mehkati hai
ho ho ho ho ho ho
kisi ke pehlu mein hum rahe khoye hue
aur aisa lage ye wadiyan usi ke geet gaati hai
ho ho ho ho ho ho*

*Door hoti hui paas aati hai
kisi ki muskaan hum ko lubhati hai
jaise dil me kamal khil gaye ho
ho ho ho ho ho ho*

*Koi khwabon mein pal pal aati hai
jo dil ki dhadhkan ko mere badhati hai
ho ho ho ho ho ho
kisi ko pal bhi nahi hue door hue
aur aisa lage usi ki yaad hum ko satati hai
ho ho ho ho ho ho*

*Door hoti hui paas aati hai
kisi ki muskaan hum ko lubhati hai
jaise dil me kamal khil gaye ho
ho ho ho ho ho ho*

6. Tejas's Love Story

Back at Kirori Mal College in Delhi, Tejas's life seemed to carry on as usual. However, his heart was filled with an unyielding longing for Sanam, and he often confided in his friends about his heartfelt feelings for her. Every time he stepped outside of the college premises, his eyes would instinctively scan the surroundings, hopeful of catching a glimpse of her presence.

In the evenings, Tejas developed a ritual of visiting a temple located near the college's back gate. There, he would fervently pray to the deities, seeking their divine intervention to help him find Sanam. It was a gesture driven by his unflagging hope that, someday, fate would unite them.

Regrettably, a few of Tejas's friends, not comprehending the intensity of his feelings, started teasing him and playfully dubbed him "Majnu Katilal." This moniker alluded to his deep yearning and was a reference to the legendary character Majnu, known for his passionate love. Despite the teasing, Tejas remained steadfast in his belief that love had the power to transcend all boundaries and that one day he would find his beloved Sanam.

In a stroke of serendipity, Tejas's heartfelt wishes were granted after a couple of weeks. One evening, as he stood outside the back gate of his college, he caught sight of a girl wearing his fleece, stepping into a rickshaw bound for Kamla Nagar Market. Filled with excitement and anticipation, Tejas decided to follow the rickshaw in the hope of reconnecting with the girl caught a glimpse of in the mighty hills.

Nonetheless, the bustling traffic and street commotion proved to be an impediment, causing the rickshaw to vanish into the throng. This left Tejas with a racing heart and a sense of nostalgia and uncertainty. It was as if all the memories from their time in Darjeeling came rushing back to him, and he could not help but wonder if it was her or perhaps someone else. Despite the disappointment, Tejas held onto the hope that he would have another chance encounter with her.

For an entire week, he faithfully returned to the same place at the same time, hoping to recreate the magical moment of their paths crossing once more. Alas, his efforts were met with no success. Nevertheless, Tejas clung to his optimism, firmly convinced that fate would reunite them. He was sanguine that someday he would get the chance to meet her, know her name, and unravel the mysteries shrouding their connection.

Every year, the college hostel organized a highly anticipated event called the Social Night. It was an occasion where girls from nearby girls' college hostels were invited to pair up with individual boys for various functions. Over the years, Tejas had gained a reputation for his stylish blazer and fashionable shoes, which had become highly sought after among the boys attending the party. Wearing Tejas's clothes seemed to bring luck, as the boys who donned them often ended up with their preferred girls as their partners.

Meanwhile, a junior-year student with rural origins had experienced a lack of success in finding a partner the year before. So, he now approached Tejas with a modest request for advice. This student had often been teased by the other boys due to his lack of success in pairing up. Touched by the student's plight, Tejas decided to take him under his wing and be his mentor for the Social Night.

Tejas generously offered his blazers and shoes to the junior student, considering them as a symbol of double luck. He not only offered the student his stylish clothing, but also shared tips and strategies to help him catch the eye of the most attractive girl and distinguish himself from the other boys. Tejas's mentoring aimed to boost the student's confidence and increase his chances of finding a compatible partner during the event.

In an interesting turn of events, for this year's Social Night event, girls from Miranda House were invited, among whom Sanam happened to be one of the most beautiful. To everyone's surprise, the junior student whom Tejas had mentored and lent his lucky attire experienced a stroke of good fortune as Sanam chose to pair up with him for the event.

However, Tejas was unaware of this development because he had decided not to participate in the event this year. Therefore, he had no knowledge of the connection between Sanam and the junior student he had mentored.

The Social Night event was taking place in the upstairs gathering room, while downstairs in the mess, dinner was being served to the non-participant boys as usual. Dinner arrangements for the participants were also set up in the upstairs gathering room. Following their meal, Tejas and his friends strolled outside the hostel toward the market. They noticed that the boys and girls in the event were walking in pairs, either entering or departing from the hostel on their way to the market.

During their conversation, Tejas' eyes were drawn to a particular pair, and he could not believe what he saw – the girl was wearing the same fleece that he had given to Sanam. Unlike before, determined not to miss this opportunity, Tejas could not contain his excitement and immediately started chasing the couple. He ran behind the girl and eventually caught up to her, placing his hand on her shoulder to stop her. To his surprise, the girl was walking with the same junior student whom Tejas had been mentoring for the event.

When the girl turned, both froze on seeing each other. A tranquil hush enveloped everything. As their gazes intertwined, it felt like time had paused. The atmosphere grew calm, and the sky's colors muted into a gentle backdrop. In that instance, all else dissolved, and Tejas and Sanam were transported to a different realm. There, it was just the two of them, captivated by the depth of their connection, unaffected by the tumult and clamor of the outside world. They were immersed in their own universe, where nothing else held significance except the profound bond they shared.

Tejas could not contain his emotions any longer and blurted out, "Honey, I have been searching for you since our last meeting. I lost you once, but I will not let you go again. I love you more than anything else, please do not leave me alone." His words poured out from the depths of his heart, filled with love and longing.

At that instant, Sanam's friends arrived, pausing to witness the evolving discussion and watch the interaction between Tejas and Sanam. Simultaneously, the less fortunate young man, who remained oblivious to the connection between Tejas and Sanam, became baffled and agitated by Tejas' actions. He felt as if his mentor was intruding and spoiling his own evening. Nonetheless, Sanam remained patient, listening attentively to Tejas as if she had been longing for him to express such sentiments for a long time. She appeared delighted, eager to respond, but before she could utter a word, the poor boy interrupted, suggesting, "Baby, let's go for some baraf (village term for ice-cream)."

Sanam, growing increasingly irritated by the poor guy's behavior, his uncouth actions, and his village-like demeanor, responded firmly, "Can you please go to the party? I will join you there."

The young man, who was less fortunate, departed the scene with a bewildered mind, trying to make sense of the situation between Sanam and Tejas. His envy toward his mentor, Tejas, skyrocketed.

The love birds reached their destination, filled with anticipation and eagerness. Similar to Tejas, Sanam had also been longing to find and meet him. Hence, whenever she left her hostel, she would don his fleece, with the hope that one day she might cross paths with the individual who had rescued her from the wrongdoers. Unbeknownst to her, she had also developed feelings for him.

As Sanam approached Tejas, she was about to say something to him, but her friends immediately intervened. Sanam attempted to convey to her friends, by pointing at her fleece, that Tejas was the person who had saved her.

However, her doubtful friend disregarded her indication and pushed Tejas aside, raising her voice to warn Sanam. She exclaimed, "I had my doubts before, Sanam, but now I am a hundred percent certain about this cheapskate. I initially thought that the misbehaving boy might be a local from Darjeeling, but now it is clear that he must have been following us from Delhi. He probably saw us in Kamla Nagar Market and has been stalking us ever since."

Sanam tried to free herself from her friend's grip and asked them, "I am not sure what you guys are talking about. Can you please explain?"

"He must be following us from Delhi and devised the incident in

Darjeeling to impress you. Do not be a fool. I know these tactics," Sanam's other friend said to her, reinforcing the doubtful narrative.

The first girl taunted Tejas, saying, "Well done, boy. Not this time...not with our girls. Try your luck somewhere else. Good luck."

The girls held Sanam's hand and escorted her away from the scene, heading toward the social event venue. They manipulated Sanam's perception of Tejas, portraying him as the villain and urging her to avoid him. Eventually, Sanam was swayed by their words and started dwelling on some anger for Tejas.

During the event, the poor boy approached Sanam as planned, hoping to spend the rest of the evening with her. However, Sanam taunted him by saying, "Did you know I prefer girls over boys? You should find another girl because I am occupied with my female sweetheart."

The unfortunate fellow felt jittery and left the venue, determined to settle the score with his mentor, Tejas.

Sanam began to believe that all the incidents were planned by Tejas as a ploy to impress her. Filled with this suspicion, she left the venue and approached a male student to return Tejas' fleece to him. Meanwhile, the poor guy also showed up, carrying Tejas' blazer and shoes, intending to give them back. He taunted Tejas, saying, "Sir, you are not a good mentor. In fact, you are a scoundrel who ruined my chance at love and a pleasant evening."

Tejas remained calm yet filled with sadness as he had once again lost someone very special to him. However, he was content to have found Sanam and had the opportunity to speak to her and learn her name and college. The junior student confronted Tejas once again, "You had promised to mentor me and gave all your lucky stuff that worked in my favor. Then why did you spoil - my party?"

Tejas sincerely begged forgiveness, intonating, "I apologize, but I have just found my long-lost love in this girl. My feelings for her are genuine, and I could not let the opportunity slip away."

The junior student mocked, saying, "Seeing a beautiful girl, you became crazy. Your friend rightly dubbed you 'Majnu Katilal.' You've gone mad; no one can save you now." Then, he took a hike.

Tejas did not want to miss the chance. Fortunately, he still had his lucky blazer and shoes with him. The poor guy had left the entry pass for the social event in the pocket of the blazer. As Tejas contemplated whether to attend the event or not, he discovered the entry pass in his blazer. This gave him a surge of confidence. Without any hesitation, he decided to seize the opportunity, put on his lucky blazer and shoes, and made his way to the social event venue.

Tejas, dressed in his formal attire, looked like a heartthrob. Sanam and her friends were taken aback to see him at the party. Although the girls were still upset with Tejas, they could not help but feel a certain attraction to this charming individual. Tejas made several attempts to approach Sanam, but she remained unresponsive.

Meanwhile, Sanam's friends had informed all the girls about Tejas' alleged plan in Darjeeling. As a result, all the girls at the party turned a blind eye to Tejas. Even Tejas' friends were criticizing him for his cheap behavior. He felt abandoned, especially under the weight of Sanam's indifference toward him.

Amid the dance party, Tejas approached the singer, grabbed the microphone, and started singing the song "*Nazaron Me Teri Aa Gaya Hun...*" in a bid to convey his emotions and catch Sanam's notice.

NAZARON ME TERI AA GAYA HUN
(*Voice*: Mr. Nazim)

Nazaron me teri aa gaya hun jo koi na koi wajah hogi sanam
nazaron me teri aa gaya hun jo koi na koi wajah hogi sanam
koi na koi wajah hogi sanam

Pyar se hi to pyar manga hai kiya nahi koi jor sanam
koi chori nahi ki hai pyar hi manga hai
wo bhi pyar se manga hai sanam

Nazaron me teri aa gaya hun jo koi na koi wajah hogi sanam
koi na koi wajah hogi sanam ..hun..hun..hun..hun..
...hun..hun..hun..hun..hun..hun...

Tor nahi koi jor nahi hai aa dil ka kar le milan (haw)
pyar me tere dil pagal hua ab tu hi bata de jayen kahan hum
wo to tu hi bata ae sanam

*Nazaron me teri aa gaya hun jo koi na koi wajah hogi sanam
koi na koi wajah hogi sanam koi na koi ..hun..hun..hun..hun..
...hun..hun..hun..hun..hun..hun...*

After his performance, Tejas intentionally left his fleece on a chair in the party hall before making his exit. Sanam, clenching the chance, asked one of her trusted friends to retrieve the fleece for her.

Tejas became restless after the incident at the social event. His friends were very concerned about him. He started visiting the Miranda House hostel and following Sanam in the Kamla Nagar Market, hoping that she would respond to his efforts and feelings. However, she consistently ignored him. Despite that, Tejas noticed that she always wore his fleece whenever he saw her. This made him believe that she still had feelings for him. One of his friends advised him, saying, "Hey man! If this girl is not responding to your feelings, then to get her attention, you should either befriend her dog or make her jealous by getting close to one of her friends."

They devised a plan on how to bring Sanam closer to Tejas. They discovered that one of their friends' sisters had enrolled in Miranda House. Fortunately, she was a close friend of Sanam and resided with her in the same hostel. She did not attend the social event at the boys' hostel, which simplified their plan. Tejas' friends persuaded him to feign friendship with the new girl, "Priya." Nevertheless, Priya's brother cautioned Tejas against toying with his sister's emotions or exploiting their friendship for personal gain. Priya agreed to assist for the sake of her brother and his friends, and the agreement was finalized.

Seizing the opportunity, Tejas assumed the role of Priya's romantic partner in igniting jealousy and discomfort in Sanam. Priya took on the role of providing Tejas with advice and hints on how to impress Sanam, acting as the intermediary between them. Within a matter of weeks, Sanam experienced sleeplessness, and emotional instability due to Priya's closeness with Tejas. Sanam attempted to approach Tejas, who intentionally ignored her on several occasions.

Frustrated, Sanam expressed to Priya that she should leave Tejas because he only had feelings for Sanam. Priya relayed this information to the boys, who were pleased to discover that their scheme was yielding results. Consequently, they intensified their efforts to undermine Sanam.

One day, Tejas accompanied Priya to an event held at her college hostel. Sanam attempted to approach Tejas, but once again, he passed over her. This was the breaking point for her. Unable to tolerate the situation any longer, she devised a plan to recreate his song from the Social Night. Sanam approached the singing and music band and began performing the song "*Nazaron Me Teri Aa Gayi Hun...*"

NAZARON ME TERI AA GAYI HUN
(*Voice*: Ms. Sadhana Sargam)

Nazaron me teri aa gayi hun jo koi na koi wajah hogi janam
nazaron me teri aa gayi hun jo koi na koi wajah hogi janam
koi na koi wajah hogi janam

Pyar se hi to pyar manga hai kia nahi koi jor janam
koi chori nahi ki hai pyar hi manga hai
wo bhi pyar se manga hai janam

Nazaron me teri aa gayi hun jo koi na koi wajah hogi janam
nazaron me teri aa gayi hun jo koi na koi wajah hogi janam
koi na koi wajah hogi janam

Tor nahi koi jor nahi hai aa dil ka kar le milan (haw)
pyar me tere dil pagal hua ab tu hi bata de jayen kahan hum
wo to tu hi bata de o janam

Nazaron me teri aa gayi hun jo koi na koi wajah hogi janam
nazaron me teri aa gayi hun jo koi na koi..hun..hun..hun..hun..
...hun..hun..hun..hun..hun..hun...

Finally, Priya recognized and acknowledged the love that existed between Tejas and Sanam. She played a crucial role in assisting them to reunite and openly express their feelings for one another. Priya forged a strong bond with both Tejas and Sanam, becoming their best friend. With Priya's support, their love story officially took flight and blossomed.

With each passing day, Tejas and Sanam's love grew stronger and more resilient. They discovered the true meaning of companionship, finding solace and happiness in each other's presence.

7. Homecoming: Tejas and Sanam

Tejas participated in the Combined Defense Services (CDS) examination with the aspiration of joining the army and dedicating himself to the service of his nation. At the time, he was in his last semester of college. On the other hand, Sanam had one more year left to finish her college studies. The army training program spanned 18 months, beginning with a year-long period in Hyderabad. Afterward, the training continued with field exercises in J&K.

Tejas and Sanam thoroughly enjoyed their time together in Delhi. Their love relationship was well-founded and committed, as they shared a deep connection. However, despite their closeness, they had not fully delved into the details of each other's life stories and backgrounds during their conversations. Nonetheless, both Tejas and Sanam nestled modern and progressive perspectives. They illustrated their open-mindedness and contemporary approach to life.

During the transition period, Tejas made the most of his break between training in Hyderabad and field training in J&K. He decided to pay a visit to his hometown. While waiting for the bus to depart from Delhi to Bareilly, he was taken aback to find Sanam boarding the same bus. Both Tejas and Sanam were filled with elation at the unexpected reunion, but their joy gradually faded as they engaged in conversation.

Their conversation led to a startling discovery – they were actually from neighboring villages that had a history of communal tensions. Occasional riots between the Hindu village and the neighboring Muslim village prevailed. This revelation brought about a deeper understanding of the complexity of their shared surroundings. Furthermore, Tejas learned that Sanam belonged to the Muslim community.

Upon learning about Sanam's Muslim background, Tejas felt fearful and apprehensive due to his firsthand experience with Hindu-Muslim communal tensions in his village. However, he consciously chose not to let his fear consume him, displaying remarkable composure and resilience. Tejas understood the importance of not alarming or distressing Sanam with his concerns regarding the communal tensions. Instead, he chose to approach the situation with care and avoid burdening Sanam with his anxieties. He aimed to preserve a sense of tranquility and stability in their relationship.

Sanam, a modern-minded individual, had not fully grasped the severity of openly acknowledging her religious identity. This stemmed from various factors in her upbringing. Although she was born into a Muslim family in a village, as an infant, she was entrusted to the care of her maternal uncle in Delhi, who happened to be a diplomat. Growing up in her uncle's household, Sanam had minimal exposure to Muslim religious practices, as her uncle's family predominantly followed Hindu customs. Her schooling and university experiences further immersed her in a typically Hindu environment.

Moreover, Sanam's parents rarely visited her, primarily due to the religious disparities between her father and her uncle. Despite these differences, her mother insisted that Sanam remain under her uncle's guardianship, resulting in limited exposure to Muslim culture in her upbringing. Consequently, Sanam's cultural, social, and educational influences were predominantly shaped by a context that did not emphasize her Muslim heritage. Thus, her decision to conceal her identity from Tejas was not a deliberate action, but rather a consequence of her circumstances and the lack of necessity to reveal her religious background.

Similarly, Tejas had never suspected that Sanam was not Hindu, as her behavior and occasional visits to temples did not indicate the contrary. Furthermore, Sanam's surname, Choudhary, was common among Hindu Jats, with only a small fraction of Muslims sharing the same surname. Consequently, her thoughts, behavior, attire, and temple visits left no room for doubt that she adhered to Hindu practices.

Zooming in back to the bus travel, due to some mechanical issues, the bus was forced to exit the highway and make a stop at a nearby gas station. The passengers were informed about the delay, which was expected to be at least an hour. Taking the opportunity, the passengers disembarked from the bus and walked over to a nearby shopping mall. While at the food court, a fellow passenger from Tejas' village recognized him, initiating a conversation. Tejas introduced Sanam to this passenger, and as they engaged in conversation, the passenger began sharing stories. However, mindful of not burdening Sanam, Tejas had refrained from discussing the communal tensions in their villages.

In the course of their conversation, the passenger shared multiple instances of conflicts that had erupted between the Hindu and Muslim-majority villages. Most of them were spurred by religious motivations. This revelation startled both Tejas and Sanam, particularly Sanam, who had been completely unaware of such incidents up until that moment. The shared episodes painted a distressing picture of the communal tensions afflicting their area. It filled them with a sense of unease about the potential difficulties they could bump into as a couple from different religious backgrounds.

Following their encounter and the revelation of Sanam's Muslim identity, Tejas and Sanam returned to their respective homes. Tejas, deeply impacted by the religious tensions between Hindus and Muslims in their villages, became anxious about the future of his relationship with Sanam. His concerns grew to the point where he distanced himself from his family, feeling isolated and saddened by the potential obstacles they might face.

Tejas's unusual behavior caught the attention of Masterji and grandma, who became genuinely concerned for him. Accustomed to seeing Tejas as an active and vibrant young man, they made earnest attempts to understand his situation and support him. Despite their efforts, Tejas kept his inner turmoil to himself, reluctant to share his fears and anxieties with his family.

One day, Masterji came across the village bus passenger who had conversed with Tejas during their unexpected meeting. Learning about Tejas's love affair with a Muslim girl from the neighboring village, both Masterji and grandma experienced a moment of fear. However, their open-hearted and broad-minded approach prevailed as they chose to understand and cooperate, recognizing the weightiness of supporting Tejas during this challenging time.

Despite understanding the potential challenges that lay ahead, Masterji and grandma were determined to help Tejas. Masterji approached Tejas and disclosed that he had become aware of Tejas' love affair with a girl from a neighboring Muslim village. Initially, they tried to reason with Tejas, expressing their concerns about the potential escalation of tension in the already volatile village environment. However, Tejas passionately asserted his deep love for Sanam and conveyed that they could not bear to be separated from each other. He went to the extent of suggesting that they consider the idea of ending their lives if their love story comes to grips with insurmountable obstacles.

Masterji, who held an immense affection for Tejas, became frightened at the thought of seeing him sad and lonely. The dilemma he faced was profound. On one hand, he valued Tejas's well-being and could not stand to witness his suffering. On the other hand, he hesitated to involve Sanam's Muslim family due to the ongoing tensions between the communities. The conflicting emotions and the weight of the decision weighed heavily on Masterji as he grappled with finding the best course of action to support Tejas and navigate the complex situation.

The passenger who had met Tejas during their bus journey chose to inform the religious leader (imam) of the Muslim village about Tejas and Sanam's love relationship. Recognizing potential religious implications and concerns, the imam took it upon himself to visit Sanam's home and caution her family about the possible consequences of a relationship beyond their religious boundaries. As a result, Sanam's family members became aware of her involvement with a Hindu boy from the neighboring village.

In the wake of the revelation about Sanam's interfaith love affair, tensions within her family escalated dramatically. Her father, being an orthodox and conservative Muslim, held strong objections to the fact that Sanam had been sent to her maternal uncle's home for education and a brighter future. Fanned by anger, he directed his frustration toward her mother, and publicly slapped her for the decision to send Sanam away. The situation quickly escalated as he exhibited irrational behavior toward the rest of the family members, creating a highly tense environment within the household.

In a fit of rage, Sanam's father swiftly decided to cut her ties with the city and enlisted the imam's help to arrange her marriage to a Muslim boy on short notice. Given her family's wealth and Sanam's beauty, the imam promptly proposed his nephew as a potential suitor for her. Against Sanam's wishes, her marriage was hastily arranged for the following month, coinciding with an auspicious date according to Muslim customs. The weight of this decision placed immense pressure on Sanam, who found herself trapped in a situation where her desires and aspirations clashed with the traditional expectations and cultural norms imposed upon her.

The news of Sanam's interfaith love affair and her impending arranged marriage to the nephew of a prominent Muslim religious leader circulated within the local community. This speedily captured sizable attention and sparked widespread interest among the residents. Tejas, already weighed down by the circumstances, grew even more restless and desperate to find a resolution. His desire to overcome all barriers and reach Sanam intensified.

Witnessing Tejas' anguish and understanding the intensity of the situation, Masterji could no longer bear to see him burdened by such overwhelming circumstances. With the aim of mediating and supporting Tejas and Sanam's love, Masterji made the challenging choice to approach Sanam's family. Recognizing the urgency and sensitivity of the matter, he embarked on a mission to seek a resolution, hoping to bridge the divide between the two families and create a path for Tejas and Sanam to be together.

Masterji, accompanied by Tejas, arrived at Sanam's house intending to engage in a conversation. However, her family members, particularly her father, adamantly refused to provide them with an opportunity to explain their perspective. Instead of allowing for dialogue, Sanam's father, joined by the imam and his nephew, resorted to both verbal and physical abuse toward Masterji. Despite Tejas' repeated attempts to shield Masterji from the mistreatment, the situation escalated.

Driven by a mixture of frustration and determination, Tejas decided to take action and began chasing away the individuals who were assaulting Masterji. However, in the chaos, an unintentional incident occurred where Sanam's father was inadvertently struck. Witnessing this, Sanam swiftly reacted, slapping Tejas and demanding that both he and Masterji leave her house immediately.

Caught off guard by the unexpected blow from Sanam, Tejas was momentarily stunned, while the other Muslim men continued their verbal abuse toward him and Masterji. They forcefully dragged them, attempting to expel them from the premises. In a pivotal moment, Masterji began singing a song titled "*Ek Kadam Tum Badhao…*" with the first part centered on promoting communal harmony. The second part was dedicated to Sanam, sung by Tejas.

<u>EK KADAM TUM BADHAO</u>
(*Voice*: Mr. Rakesh Singh & Arvind Ojha)

*Ek kadam tum badhao hun hun hun hun hun……
ek kadam tum badhao sau kadam aaye hain hum
ek kadam tum badhao sau kadam aaye hain hum
{aao miljul kar rahein kar dein ab chaino aman
ek kadam tum badhao sau kadam aaye hain hum
ek kadam tum badhao sau kadam aaye hain hum}x2*

*Mere chale jaane se agar yahan koi fark pade
mere chale jaane se agar yahan koi fark pade
hans ke sab ke liye yahan mit jayenge hum
yehi wada hai mera aaj kahte hain hum*

Ek kadam tum badhao sau kadam aaye hain hum

*Aao hum milkar karein pyar ka ailan sanam
ek kadam tum badhao sau kadam aaye hain hum
ek kadam tum badhao sau kadam aaye hain hum*

*Ek ishara kar do to tare tor layenge
ek ishara kar do to tare tor layenge
pyar tumhe itna karun jitna kabhi soche na tum
samajh na aaye yakin kar le humpe humdum*

*Ek kadam tum badhao sau kadam aaye hain hum
ek kadam tum badhao sau kadam aaye hain hum
aao hum milkar karein pyar ka ailan sanam
ek kadam tum badhao sau kadam aaye hain hum
aao miljul kar rahein kar dein ab chaino aman
aao miljul kar rahein kar dein ab chaino aman*

At the conclusion of the song, Sanam and her family remained silent, offering no response to Tejas and Masterji's plea for understanding. Accepting the reality that their efforts had been in vain, both Tejas and Masterji made the tough decision to leave the Muslim village behind and return to grandma's school. It was within the comforting walls of the school that they sought solace and support in the aftermath of the turbulent events.

Tejas, consumed by anger and disappointment at Sanam's and her family's behavior, particularly the abuse suffered by Masterji, chose to sever his ties with Sanam. He conveyed his choice to both Masterji and grandma, stating that their efforts had been satisfactory and that he had moved beyond the incident at Sanam's house. At that moment, Tejas desired to create distance between himself, Sanam, and the village environment. He deciphered that his selfish pursuit of the love affair had only brought disgrace and harm to himself and Masterji. Tejas also disclosed his plan to resume his military training in a few days, aiming to refocus his attention and leave behind the painful memories that had transpired.

At home, Sanam found herself discontented with how her family had treated the Hindu men, including Tejas and Masterji. Furthermore, she was deeply saddened and angered by her impending marriage to the imam's nephew, a union that went against her own wishes. Despite her turmoil, she had no one to confide in and share her feelings with. While her mother had initially supported her by sending her to the city, she now appeared helpless in the face of the situation. Moreover, her mother had reservations about Sanam being involved with a Hindu boy like Tejas.

However, after two days, Sanam's mother began showing some sympathy toward her, considering the deteriorating state of Sanam's health. This brought a glimmer of courage to Sanam's heart. Yet, it remained uncertain whether her mother would support her relationship with Tejas. Sanam's mother wrestled with conflicting thoughts about Muslim religious practices. She harbored discontent over the practice of polygamy, as her own husband had married a young girl the same age as Sanam and brought her into their household. She was worried that her daughter might face a similar fate, as she was to be wed to the nephew of an orthodox imam, who himself had three wives living in the same house. Sanam's mother was torn about her husband's hasty decision regarding their daughter's marriage.

Ultimately, she made a courageous choice. Sanam's mother decided to help her daughter escape from the tense and suffocating environment they were in and beat a retreat to the city. In a private conversation, she revealed her plan to Sanam, assuring her support. Sanam felt a renewed sense of hope as if she had been given a second chance at life. However, she could not gather the courage to ask her mother for permission to elope with Tejas. Her mother advised her to behave normally to avoid arousing suspicion among the rest of the family. She assured her that once the situation had normalized, she would signal for her to run away. Although Sanam tried her best to act normal, she still felt suffocated within the tense environment of her family.

One fine afternoon, as Sanam found herself feeling lonely, she sought solace in the serene mango orchard near a bushy pond. She recalled the moments spent with Tejas, especially their happy days in Delhi when one day they enjoyed a live concert of singer Richa Sharma, who performed a sad, heart-touching song. Immersed in her sorrowful state, she began singing a poignant song, "*Kisne Kaha Teri Yaad...*," expressing the depth of her longing. The melody resonated through the orchard, carrying her emotions with each heartfelt note. In that melancholic moment, surrounded by nature's embrace, Sanam found a brief escape from the burdens that weighed upon her.

KISNE KAHA TERI YAAD
(*Voice*: Ms. Richa Sharma & (Ms. Khushboo Jain))
Kisne kaha teri yaad na aayegi
teri yaad hi to hum ko satayegi
teri yaad hi to hum ko satayegi

kisne kaha teri yaad na aayegi
teri yaad hi to hum ko satayegi, hum ko satayegi

Kisne kaha teri yaad na aayegi
teri yaad hi to hum ko rulayegi, hum ko rulayegi
dil ne kaha teri hi yaad aayegi
tere pyar me hi to umar beet jayegi
tujh se door hoke jana jaan chali jayegi, jaan chali jayegi

Kisne kaha teri yaad na aayegi
teri yaad hi to hum ko tadpayegi, hum ko tadpayegi
dil ne kaha teri hi yaad aayegi
teri yaad me hi to zindagi jayegi
(phir bhi) teri khushi ki dil me tamanna rahegi, tamanna rahegi

Kisne kaha teri yaad na aayegi
teri yaad hi to hum ko satayegi, hum ko satayegi
aa aa aa a… aa aa aa a…
(hun hun hun hu…hun hun hun hu…)
aa aa aa a… aa aa aa a…
(hun hun hun hu…hun hun hun hu…)

Masterji, as he passed by the mango orchard, was drawn to Sanam's heartfelt singing from the very beginning. Intrigued, he concealed himself under the sheltering bushes, listening intently to the emotions conveyed in her song. As the last note hung in the air, a photograph, seemingly carried by fate, landed in front of Masterji, affirming his belief that the song was dedicated to Tejas.

Realizing the depth of Sanam's love for Tejas and her willingness to endure her sadness for his happiness, Masterji resolved to have a one-on-one conversation with her regarding their situation. After a while, he approached Sanam and expressed his apologies for interfering in her family matters. He emphasized his rock-solid love for Tejas and his commitment to their happiness. Masterji assured her that he stood by their side and encouraged her to share her true desires for her relationship with Tejas. Aware that the Muslim family would not likely approve, Masterji posed a direct question, "Will you run away with Tejas? I am here to assist you both, but I need your permission."

Masterji's words brought a sense of relief to Sanam. Although initially bashful, she recognized that Masterji's suggestion was the only viable path for their love.

Overwhelmed with emotion, she poured her heart out to Masterji, sharing her innermost feelings. In their conversation, Sanam revealed that her mother, at some point, had expressed a desire for her to escape the village, potentially seeking refuge with her uncle in the city. However, she was unsure if her mother would support her in eloping with Tejas. Masterji encouraged her to express her feelings to her mother, hoping for a positive response. He assured her that he would send a trusted nurse as a messenger, facilitating Sanam's communication of her ultimate decision and, with her mother's consent, organizing their escape.

With Masterji's guidance and the indirect support of Sanam's mother, a plan was devised. Sanam successfully fled from her home, and Masterji conveyed the same to Tejas. Masterji made all the necessary arrangements for their marriage to take place in a nearby city, at the house of a trusted friend. The wedding ceremony was a beautiful fusion of both Hindu and Muslim rituals, honoring their respective traditions and symbolizing the union of their love and cultures.

Masterji understood the potential consequences of going against the wishes of the Muslim family. Prior to Tejas and Sanam's departure for J&K, where Tejas had to resume his military training, Masterji had a serious conversation with Tejas. He requested Tejas to make a solemn promise that under no circumstances would he return to the village, even upon receiving news of Masterji's or grandma's passing. Tejas initially hesitated to make such a difficult promise, but after heartfelt pleas from Masterji, he reluctantly agreed to honor Masterji's request. It was a bittersweet moment for Tejas, as he accepted the promise, knowing that it meant sacrificing his ability to visit the village for the sake of their marriage, all based on Masterji's insistence.

In the midst of the chaotic and urgent moment, Tejas's grandma, filled with boundless love and pride, had nothing but her heartfelt blessings to offer. She clasped a bravery medal, posthumously bestowed upon her son by the Indian government for his courageous service in the army, and tenderly fastened it around Tejas's neck. With a thick film of tears, she offered her support and blessings as Tejas continued his military journey, carrying the legacy of courage and sacrifice that coursed through their family.

8. Outbreak of Communal Riots

The village's atmosphere grew increasingly fraught after Sanam's escape from home. It was soon discovered that Tejas was also missing from the village at the same time. This sparked off the villagers' suspicion that Tejas had lured Sanam away with him. The impetus at that time was to locate Sanam and Tejas, with the Muslim community being strongly motivated by the desire for revenge against Tejas. They eagerly awaited an opportunity to find both of them. The head of the Muslim community even issued a fatwa against Tejas. Despite the passage of four months, no clues were found to trace their whereabouts.

Tejas's military training was conducted covertly, making it extremely challenging to determine his location. Despite the Muslims' attempts to intimidate Masterji into divulging information about Tejas, their efforts proved futile. The orthodox Hindus remained watchful, ensuring the protection of Masterji and his school, as they feared the potential backlash from the enraged Muslim community. The imam managed to persuade some troublemakers in the Muslim community that Masterji was involved in aiding the elopement of the young couple.

During the panchayat hearing, Masterji adeptly presented Tejas as a compliant and obedient individual. He claimed that after the humiliation Tejas faced at the Muslim family's doorstep, Tejas chose to avoid any further discussion or involvement in his relationship with the Muslim girl. Furthermore, Tejas made the independent decision to cut off all contact with her and leave the village due to his involvement in a confidential government mission. That undertaking prohibited him from seeking information or disclosing his whereabouts. Being fully aware of the gravity of the government mission, Masterji respected the boundaries and refrained from prying into Tejas' location or pursuing further inquiries. While some in the Muslim community accepted Masterji's explanation, a faction, including the imam, remained skeptical and questioned the truth of his statements.

The imam was suspicious that Masterji had a hand in Tejas and Sanam's break-out. He was hatching a conspiracy to harm Masterji, aiming to seek revenge. They hadn't located Tejas yet, but the imam was driven by his doubts. He desired revenge and planned to target Masterji.

As part of their scheme, they spread a false rumor that Tejas would be returning to the village school. The intention behind this misinformation was to lure Masterji into a vulnerable position where they could carry out their attack. However, unknown to them, Tejas had actually been selected for a highly classified government mission.

Simultaneously, Tejas had been chosen to join an army team for a top-secret assignment along the India-Pakistan border in J&K. His mission involved capturing a notorious militant chief who posed a threat in the region. Oblivious to the rumors and conspiracy swirling in his village, Tejas set sail on this dangerous assignment, fully committed to serving his country.

Meanwhile, in the village, the orthodox Muslims, believing the false rumor about Tejas's return, departed to attack Masterji's school, seeking revenge for Tejas eloping with the Muslim girl. However, unbeknownst to them, Tejas was already on his way to the border with the army team for his secret mission. These two events— the planned attack on Masterji's school and Tejas's departure for the border— coincided, unfolding simultaneously without any direct connection.

A small group of Muslims attacked Masterji's school, facing some resistance from the Hindu volunteers guarding the premises. Unfortunately, the number of Hindus was significantly outnumbered by the Muslim mob. During the course of this chaotic situation, a 7-year-old Muslim child, who had been playing near the school, got caught in the thick of the violent clash. The child cried out in distress as he sustained injuries from the violent clashes between the Hindus and Muslims, particularly from the pelting of stones.

Masterji saw the child in distress. The child was dressed in Muslim attire and needed help. Masterji swiftly recognized the danger from a couple of approaching Hindu men who were unaware of the child's presence. In a brave move to protect the vulnerable child from harm and prevent further injuries, Masterji stepped forward and discreetly sheltered the child under his shawl. He wanted to ensure the child's safety and make him less noticeable to the approaching Hindu individuals.

However, from a distance, a Muslim man observed Masterji's actions and misinterpreted his intentions. Falsely suspecting that Masterji was causing harm to the Muslim child by suffocating him under the shawl, the man fired a gun at Masterji in an attempt to free the child from his perceived captivity.

The gunshot struck Masterji, penetrating the back of his head and reaching his forehead, causing him to collapse instantaneously. Meanwhile, as the child emerged from underneath the shawl, he noticed that Masterji was bleeding from the gunshot wound. Looking around, he noticed his uncle holding the fired gun and beckoning the boy to come toward him.

In response, the child vehemently questioned his uncle's actions, demanding to know why he had killed Masterji, who had been protecting him from the approaching hostile Hindu individuals. With a firm resolve, the child declared that he would not go to his uncle, recognizing his uncle's malevolence, and instead chose to stay and assist Masterji.

The child did his best to assist the fallen Masterji, providing whatever aid he could. Despite his injuries, Masterji made eye contact with the child and attempted to speak, uttering, "Hey God, please forgive me for any sins I may have committed," before his breath ceased, and he succumbed to his wounds.

The resounding gunshot, Masterji's sudden collapse, and the poignant plea of the child to his Muslim uncle resonated among the approaching Hindus and the onlookers nearby. In a moment of heightened emotions, the Hindus quickly pursued the accused Muslim man, carrying out their form of vengeance through a brutal act of lynching, leading to his immediate death.

Following the tragic demise of Masterji, a wave of communal violence erupted, plunging the area into chaos. As the evening set in, an alarming number of Hindus, estimated to be over ten thousand, surrounded the small Muslim village from three sides. The fourth side was left unguarded because some Hindu families resided in that area of the village.

As the attack on the Muslim village by the Hindus became apparent, the neighboring Muslim populations who had friendly relations with the Hindus on the fourth side of the village quickly sought refuge and concealment from the supportive Hindus. These friendly Hindus extended their support by hiding and sheltering the Muslim neighbors, ensuring their safety.

However, apart from the Muslim residents who found shelter among their friendly Hindu counterparts, the majority of the village's Muslim population, including women and children, were forcefully taken out of their homes and paraded in an open field.

The Muslims were coerced into identifying those responsible for inciting communal tensions. They were warned that if anyone attempted to protect the culprits, the entire Muslim community would face consequences. Women and young children were particularly threatened, with the possibility of harm to their loved ones if they tried to intervene. Scared for their lives, they started narrating the stories of whatever they knew about the hatched conspiracy and the culprits behind that. The bad guys were isolated. The women and juveniles were asked to return home.

A second round of filtration was initiated among the isolated Muslim individuals to identify the true culprits and masterminds behind the heinous act. Extensive investigations were carried out, and after careful scrutiny, a list of individuals involved in the incident was compiled.

The graveness of the situation called for swift and decisive action. It was decided that those identified as the real perpetrators would face the most severe form of punishment: the death penalty. This decision aimed to send a strong message and instill fear in the Muslim community. It served as a deterrent against future attempts to disrupt peace and harmony between Hindus and Muslims.

The execution of the death penalty was carried out promptly, leaving no room for delay. The objective was to demonstrate the zero-tolerance approach toward those who threatened the unity and integrity of the region. By taking immediate and firm action, the hope was that the message would resonate widely, emphasizing the need for communal harmony and discouraging religious or communal animosity.

While the decision to execute the death penalty may have been viewed as harsh by some, it was deemed necessary to preserve the fragile fabric of interfaith relations and to prevent any escalation of violence or retribution. The intention was not to target the entire Muslim community, but rather to root out the individuals responsible for perpetuating the crime and to ensure that justice was served.

The news of Masterji's demise was rapidly spreading, and simultaneously, the execution of the death penalty for the Muslim perpetrators became widely known in the nearby villages. This news particularly affected the Muslim villages, which had a population of around twenty thousand people, as many of them had relatives among those who were executed.

At midnight, a horde of around four thousand enraged Muslims retaliated by launching a violent attack on the Hindu village. The assailants showed no mercy as they ruthlessly slaughtered thirty-eight individuals, including women and children. The violence extended beyond human lives, as they also targeted and mercilessly slaughtered the village's livestock and cattle.

The attack continued until the Hindu residents, faced with the gravity of the situation and determined to protect their lives and property, took up arms and offered gun resistance. This unexpected show of resistance from the Hindus caught the attackers off guard, causing them to retreat from the village.

Unfortunately, the emergence of communal tensions occurred at an inopportune time. It coincided with the Dussehra celebrations taking place throughout the region, with the following day being the eve of Vijayadashami. In various parts of the area, towering effigies of Ravana, symbolizing evil, were being prepared for burning along with firework displays aimed at vanquishing evil. Additionally, the processions for the immersion of goddess Durga's idol were underway. Therefore, Hindus were outside of their homes everywhere. They were excited and enticed to gather in melas (fairs). Most Hindus were traditionally armed for the celebration of

Dussehra. The atmosphere was filled with anticipation and joy as families came together to commemorate the victory of good over evil.

Due to past incidents of Hindu provocation against Muslims, the Muslim community had prepared themselves for any unforeseen situation. This readiness resulted from the presence of orthodox or provocative Hindu crowds during the Ravana Dahan ritual and the procession for the immersion of goddess Durga's idol. Muslims were armed, vigilant, and monitoring the situation to protect themselves.

In the past, both conservative Hindus and orthodox Muslims had chanted outrageous slogans during processions to offend the sentiments of the other community. Such provocative acts had resulted in scattered incidents of communal violence in the past. However, these situations were typically managed peacefully through the efforts of the administration and collaborative initiatives by the communities. However, these incidents revealed that communal tensions persisted during religious gatherings. This necessitated vigilance and readiness from both communities and the administration.

However, nobody could have anticipated that the communal riot would escalate to such a widespread and terrifying level, spiraling out of control for the administration. The news of Masterji's killing by Muslims, the subsequent punishment meted out to the orthodox Muslim perpetrators by the Hindus, and the retaliatory massacre of Hindus by Muslims rapidly spread throughout the region like wildfire.

As people were already prepared, agitated, and armed, they began organizing for revenge against the opposing communities. Spontaneously, several Muslim villages were attacked and torched; resulting in the mass killing of Muslim men, women, elderly individuals, young people, and even children. The scale of the massacres was devastating, resulting in the loss of a significant portion of the Muslim population as well as some Hindus. In just a single day, nearly five percent of the Muslim population, along with a number of Hindus, was tragically wiped out.

The enormity of the violence and its impact on the affected communities was staggering. A strict curfew was imposed in the whole region. Still, the mob was out of control and widespread communal violence was uncontrolled by the administration. Instantly, the army was called but it was too late to save at least ten percent of the population. The whole region was under fire for at least four days. This communal riot was one of the worst in the entire recent history of the country.

Rita learned about the intensity of the riot through her media team. As she received news of Masterji's tragic demise, she could not help but feel a pang of sorrow for the loss. Despite any differences they may have had, she still held a soft spot for him in her heart. Understanding the gravity of the situation, Rita decided to personally cover the news.

Amidst stringent security measures, Rita took to the skies and joined her team at the scene. Determined to provide comprehensive coverage, she actively participated in press coverage alongside her team. However, her purpose extended beyond mere reporting. Rita's quest also involved digging out the underlying reasons behind Masterji's untimely death.

Driven by a combination of professional responsibility and a personal connection, Rita devoted herself to delving deeper into the circumstances of the killing. With a commitment to unmasking the truth, she engaged in investigative journalism, conducting interviews and seeking information that would shed light on the root cause of Masterji's tragic fate.

Rita's venture into the heart of the situation brought her face-to-face with the harsh realities of the riot. Despite the risks and challenges that lay ahead, she remained resolute in her pursuit of justice and in unraveling the truth behind the loss of Masterji.

John was on his business trip to Delhi. He saw the televised news broadcasting about the situation in his village. He was shell-shocked to learn about Masterji's demise and the communal riots in his village. John immediately rushed to his village. While he was traveling back home, all the memories of the village with Masterji projected as a film reel. He remembered his friendship with Masterji and how Masterji helped him settle down in the village. John recalled how Masterji and the rest of the villagers, including Hindus and Muslims, were depending on him for the daily radio news broadcast.

Both communities respected him. John lived somewhere in the middle of both villages and adjacent to Masterji's school. He was the only one with a loudspeaker to daily broadcast radio news to the villagers. Thus, John was the only source of daily national news for the villagers. Every evening, many villagers gathered on his doorsteps to listen to the news broadcast and read the newspapers. Those who stayed at home also enjoyed the daily radio news broadcast at 8.30 p.m.

Returning home, John promptly activated his loudspeaker, not for broadcasting news, but for a more cardinal purpose. He voiced a heartfelt speech about his choice to relocate from another country and make this community his home, even when he could have explored other parts of India. John shared his personal experiences and the reasons that made him feel secure in this neighborhood as a lone Christian man amidst people from various communities.

Foremost, John spoke about himself, highlighting his journey and the warmth and acceptance he had received from the community. He emphasized the central role played by a remarkable man who had not only helped him but also inspired him to embrace life in the village—Masterji. With deep admiration and respect, John delved into Masterji's love story and the story of Tejas's upbringing.

He recounted the tale of Masterji, an extraordinary individual who had experienced heartbreak when he was abandoned by a woman from the city whom he deeply loved. Despite this setback, Masterji's compassion knew no bounds. He went on to raise an unknown child, whom he found discarded in a dumpster at the city's railway station. This child, later named Tejas, became Masterji's own, and Masterji chose to remain unmarried for the sake of his son.

John's words resonated with the villagers, as he recounted the selfless acts and sacrifices made by Masterji. But the most significant sacrifice of all came when Masterji laid down his own life in an attempt to save a Muslim child, who belonged to a different religious community. This revelation left the villagers in awe, for they had never known the true identity of Tejas or the circumstances surrounding Masterji's heroic act.

With a fervent plea, John asked the villagers if anyone could shed light on the origins of the baby that Masterji had discovered. He implored them to consider whether the child, Tejas, was Hindu, Muslim, Sikh, or Christian—a poignant reminder that Masterji had given up his life to protect a child without any regard for religious differences.

Continuing his impassioned address, John reminded the villagers of Masterji's tireless efforts to bridge the communal divide between the Hindu and Muslim communities. Through his dedication to education, mediation, counseling, and social work, Masterji had successfully nurtured an atmosphere of peace and harmony between the two communities. It was Masterji's enduring efforts that had allowed both communities to coexist peacefully for many years.

In a stern tone, John laid blame on the collective ignorance of the villagers, regardless of their religious affiliations. He held them accountable for the loss of a person who had become the embodiment of communal harmony and peace. John implored them to learn from Masterji's sacrifice and to honor his memory by extending prayers for peace and the well-being of his soul. Masterji's commitment to communal harmony was evident through raising an unknown child, Tejas, as his own and his ultimate sacrifice to protect a child from a different religious community.

John's words hung heavy in the air, stirring emotions and igniting a sense of responsibility among the villagers. They realized the relevance of their actions and the impact they had on their beloved Masterji. The community experienced deep introspection, pondering their collective responsibility to uphold the ideals of peace, harmony, and unity that Masterji had tirelessly advocated. This helped to break off the communal riot instantly.

In the aftermath of John's passionate speech, a solemn silence settled over the village. The realization of their past actions and the consequences they bore weighed heavily on their hearts. The way forward became evident: they needed to glean wisdom from Masterji's sacrifices, water communal harmony, and strive to build unity and understanding among all members of their community.

United by a shared sense of purpose, the villagers resolved to honor Masterji's legacy. They pledged to abolish the barriers that divided them, to set aside their differences, and to forge a path of harmony and cooperation. The villagers decided to build a statue of

Masterji at the chowk as a symbol of unity and communal harmony. The memory of Masterji and his untiring commitment to communal harmony would serve as a guiding light, reminding them of the importance of love, acceptance, and compassion.

From that day forward, the village ventured into a transformative odyssey. The residents actively sought opportunities to bridge gaps, build bridges of understanding, and create an inclusive environment that celebrated diversity. They established forums for dialogue, organized cultural exchanges, and implemented educational programs aimed at fostering mutual respect and appreciation.

As time passed, the village began to heal. The wounds inflicted by ignorance and prejudice slowly gave way to a renewed sense of belonging and shared humanity. The legacy of Masterji, carried forth by John's impassioned speech, became the catalyst for positive change and a testament to the indomitable spirit of unity.

In the years that followed, the village transformed into a beacon of communal harmony, attracting visitors from far and wide who sought to learn from their journey. Their tale of redemption and shared development inspired neighboring communities and beyond, emphasizing the influence of love and understanding in surmounting divisions and building a more inclusive society.

Thus, the village welcomed a future where Masterji's legacy endured, communal harmony flourished, and the wisdom gained from the sacrifices made for the common good was engraved in the hearts and minds of all its residents.

Rita, upon receiving the news from John's broadcast, was utterly devastated by the harsh reality that emerged before her. As she reflected on her actions, the burden of regret grew heavier in her heart. She comprehended the depth of the pain she had inflicted upon Masterji, a man of kindness and integrity. The knowledge that he had loved her deeply and remained unmarried until his last breath filled her with profound remorse for the insults and abandonment she had subjected him to.

The depth of her sorrow deepened as she learned about the selfless acts of kindness performed by Masterji. He had not only saved an orphan child, but had also raised the child as his own, exemplifying his unconditional love and compassion. Rita came to understand the immense sacrifices he had made, putting the child's well-being above his own.

The most heart-wrenching tragedy that dawned upon her was the realization that Masterji, a Hindu by faith, had sacrificed his life to shield a Muslim child from the grasp of Hindu orthodoxy. The sheer magnitude of this selfless act shattered Rita. It left her battling with the enormity of the loss and the deep love that Masterji had exemplified, transcending the boundaries of religion.

Overwhelmed with emotions, Rita found herself in crossfire with a sense of guilt and remorse. The consequences of her actions became all too apparent as she comprehended the depths of the pain inflicted upon the person she had once loved and still held a deep affection for.

Rita's heart was filled with a compound of grief, regret, and a renewed understanding of the love that Masterji had bestowed upon her and the child. It was a painful awakening to the impact of her choices and the irreversible loss she had inadvertently caused.

9. Masterji's Past: John's Narrative

Masterji's father held the rank of an army brigadier and was stationed in Leh-Ladakh. During an expedition in the Leh region, militants targeted his father's convoy, resulting in the tragic loss of both his parents. Masterji, however, miraculously survived the attack, albeit with a severe head injury. It was his grandmother (grandma) who stepped in to provide care and support for him. At the time of the incident, Masterji was just 5 years old.

His grandma, driven by a deep sense of social service, ran a school dedicated to providing free education for underprivileged children. She funded this noble endeavor through her life savings and the annuity compensation received from her late husband. The grandma held a strong desire for her family members to serve the nation and join the Indian army, wishing for more descendants to follow in their footsteps.

During his formative years, Masterji found refuge in his grandma's school, where he received his education up until middle school. He completed his high school studies in a neighboring village. As he excelled academically, he received a prestigious opportunity to pursue a bachelor's degree in German studies at JNU in Delhi.

Masterji's fascination with computer languages ignited during his childhood, and his interest continued to gather mass during his time in Delhi. Initially, he enrolled in computer software development courses at a coaching institute near JNU. It was there that he had the good fortune of crossing paths with a brilliant professor of Computer Science from the esteemed IIT, who often visited the coaching institute.

Recognizing Masterji's exceptional aptitude for computer technology, the professor extended a generous offer of free guidance and access to the laboratory facilities at IIT. After completing his daily studies at JNU, Masterji started dedicating his free time to the IIT laboratories, using the off hours to diligently cultivate his software development skills. With the professor and his team providing mentorship and guidance, Masterji's growth in the field was nothing short of remarkable.

In an astonishingly short timeframe, Masterji rose to become one of the premier software developers, surpassing the skills of numerous PhD holders in computer science from IIT. His innate talent was truly extraordinary, with none able to match his exceptional capabilities. Despite being an undergraduate arts student, Masterji's prowess far exceeded that of engineers hailing from IIT.

Masterji, with his exceptional intellect, holds the distinction of being the sole individual in the world to have devised a software blueprint in the 1990s. This blueprint entailed the numerical representation of four digits, specifically designed to denote the complete numerical value of years starting from the year 2000. Masterji astutely restricted the validity of the software code to a period of five years at a time. Beyond that duration, re-validation and re-coding were deemed necessary.

Given its immense popularity and the limited five-year lifespan, numerous private companies were willing to offer exorbitant sums to secure a monopoly over the software. However, during this time, Masterji became acutely aware of the selfish and self-serving nature of the contracting company. Therefore, he chose to code the software for only five years, allowing him to reevaluate and renegotiate the terms and conditions under the evolving circumstances.

From a young age, Masterji had a deep-seated desire to serve his country as a soldier in the esteemed Indian army. Regrettably, his aspirations were hindered by the lingering effects of his severe head injury, rendering him ineligible to qualify in the rigorous selection process. Undeterred by this setback, Masterji sought an alternative path to contribute to the nation's defense. Leveraging his exceptional software expertise, he firmly resolved to contribute his skills and knowledge to the research and development divisions of the Indian Defense Ministry. Therefore, he provided his services on a voluntary basis without any charge. In doing so, Masterji found a way to fulfill his innate desire to serve the Indian army and his beloved nation.

Masterji had an unparalleled mastery in software development that could have garnered him immense wealth, potentially amounting to billions of dollars. However, his priorities transcended monetary gains. Money held little allure for Masterji as his true calling lay in serving the community and his beloved nation. He placed greater value on utilizing his exceptional skills for the betterment of society, eschewing personal wealth in favor of selfless dedication to his country and its people.

As Masterji had a unique technique unmatched by anyone else in the world, he faced extreme pressure from numerous organizations, including private companies, seeking his assistance. Despite the lucrative opportunities that lay before him, Masterji made a conscious decision not to sell his skills and technology outright. Instead, he opted to license them for a limited period to select private companies.

With the earnings he amassed through licensing, Masterji set foot on a noble endeavor. He established a welfare organization dedicated to providing assistance to injured and retired army personnel, as well as the families of deceased army personnel. This organization aimed to alleviate the struggles faced by those who had sacrificed for their country.

In addition to his philanthropic efforts, Masterji also utilized a portion of the funds to sustain his grandma's school and engage in local community service. By allocating resources to these causes, he ensured that education and community development remained integral aspects of his mission.

Following Masterji's unfortunate demise, private companies resorted to desperate measures in their pursuit of his computer and software discovery assets. They dispatched their hired goons and representatives to seize Masterji's valuable possessions, hoping to claim his groundbreaking work as their own. However, their nefarious efforts were thwarted.

In a surprising turn of events, John, who had initially been lured into the conspiracy, experienced a change of heart. Recognizing the injustice thickening before him, he resolved to take a stand for justice and support Masterji's family and the community. Acting swiftly, John devised a plan to safeguard Masterji's belongings.

With utmost care, John discreetly concealed Masterji's valuable assets in the humble abode of a poverty-stricken individual. By entrusting the items to this unsuspecting benefactor, he ensured their safety from the prying eyes of the unscrupulous private companies.

In a further act of defiance, John deliberately provided false information to the representatives of these companies. By doing so, he effectively misled them, barricading the crucial information within the protective confines of the community. The private companies, despite their relentless pursuit, were ultimately unable to achieve their malicious objectives.

John's commitment to justice and his allegiance to Masterji's legacy ensured the preservation of the relevant information and assets within the community that held Masterji in high regard.

Masterji had made meticulous arrangements for the inheritance of all his groundbreaking inventions. He designated Tejas as the rightful heir, ensuring that upon his demise, Tejas would automatically assume ownership of the intellectual property. However, should Tejas also pass away, the responsibility and rights would naturally be transferred to his spouse.

In this arrangement, whenever Tejas' wife visited the village, all matters related to Masterji's discoveries were dutifully handed to her. She held the rightful authority to own, manage, and engage in contractual agreements with any company she deemed fit.

After being abandoned by Rita at the railway station, Masterji made a conscious decision not to seek a livelihood elsewhere. Instead, he dedicated himself to the betterment of the local community and the welfare of the Indian army. He achieved this by leveraging his software contracts and licensing agreements, ensuring that the proceeds served meaningful purposes.

A crucial aspect of Masterji's commitment was providing his software free of charge to the research and development wing of the Indian defense organization. By doing so, he played a pivotal role in modernizing the technological support systems for the Indian army, facilitating their efficiency and effectiveness in safeguarding the nation.

Masterji also helped grandma in managing the local school, contributing to the educational development of the community and ensuring access to education for the village's children. His goal was to empower the younger generation with knowledge and opportunities for growth.

The earnings generated from his software ventures were also allocated toward various welfare initiatives. This encompassed providing aid to the local community, bolstering healthcare services, and supporting the welfare of the Indian army organization. Through these endeavors, Masterji sought to uplift the village and its inhabitants, promoting progress and well-being.

In addition to his philanthropic pursuits, Masterji took on the responsibility of raising Tejas as his own son. This compassionate act reflected his sincere desire to create a nurturing environment for the young boy and guide him toward a promising future.

In essence, Masterji's dedication to the welfare of the community, the Indian army, and the education of future generations remained steadfast. His selflessness and commitment to noble causes left an indelible mark on the village, making a notable difference in the lives of those he touched.

Masterji's original name was Manmohan. Upon his return to the village after completing his studies at JNU, he wholeheartedly dedicated himself to serving the community and assumed the role of an efficient administrator at his grandma's school. One day, a college friend visited him and shared with the villagers how Manmohan's supportive nature, particularly in the realm of education, had earned him the endearing title of "Masterji." The villagers, already inspired by his selfless service, were captivated by the praise and recognition, and they too began referring to him as "Masterji." This name became synonymous with his commitment to education, community welfare, and his invaluable contributions to the village.

On his very first day at JNU, Masterji became the target of mockery from a group of girls who found amusement in his rural attire and his long, oil-draining hair. Among the individuals joining in the laughter was a girl named Rita Sirohi. Rita, a modern yet spoiled Jat girl, hailed from a family of immense wealth. Her family was known as one of the wealthiest industrialist families, boasting numerous diversified business portfolios. These included a highly acclaimed media branch that encompassed TV channels and newspapers.

Masterji found himself in an unfortunate situation while visiting a street vendor near the corner of the library. As he approached the vendor to buy some snacks, a group of girls began teasing him, deliberately causing him to lose his balance and stumble onto the sloping road. This resulted in his belongings scattering all over the place.

Determined to regain his composure, Masterji stooped to collect his things. Some girls, perhaps realizing the extent of their actions, stepped forward to lend a helping hand. However, others mischievously engaged in a game of hide and seek with his belongings, making it difficult for him to retrieve them. Amidst the chaos, Masterji's attention became fixated on a girl named Rita.

Rita, while continuing to ridicule him, also displayed a hint of kindness by assisting in the retrieval of his scattered items. A cord became entangled with Masterji, and an irresistible attraction magnetized him toward her. Unbeknownst to Masterji, his fascination with Rita did not escape the notice of the other girls, who observed his unwavering attention. With remarkable agility, he adeptly freed himself from the entanglement, swiftly retrieved his scattered belongings, and ran for the hills.

The next day, Masterji arrived for his German class and settled on a vacant seat. After some time, he began to hear teasing sounds emanating from the back row. Uncertain of the source of these comments, which echoed the previous day's incidents, he turned around to investigate. To his astonishment, he discovered that Rita and her mischievous gang of girls occupied the back bench, seemingly seizing every chance to torment him. Though Rita assumed the role of their leader, Masterji demonstrated remarkable patience and found himself gradually growing more tolerant of her disruptive behavior.

The girls made certain assumptions about the young man, presuming that he came from a lower economic background and had possibly gained admission through the reserved SC & ST category. They speculated that he would likely fail the semester, leading to his expulsion from the university. Some of them openly taunted him with remarks like, "Hey, Mr. Gentleman! Enjoy your scholarship and free meals at JNU while you can. We all know what will happen to you after the first semester exams. Better get ready to have your belongings thrown out by the administration!"

Being abashed by that group of girls was like enduring a storm of relentless whispers, each word a chilling raindrop of mockery that soaked Masterji's spirit.

With time, the girls' perception of Masterji transformed remarkably. They soon realized that he had exceptional intelligence and had earned the favor of the college professors. Not only that, but Masterji also displayed a remarkable level of cooperation and helpfulness. His class notes were meticulous, comprehensive, and extensively researched, making them an invaluable resource for his peers. The male students, in particular, relied heavily on his class notes, considering them to be the most beneficial study material available.

Masterji's willingness to share his class notes and his natural leadership and teaching abilities earned him the endearing nickname "Masterji." He went the extra mile to assist his fellow students, offering them essential guidance and resources for academic excellence. The impact of his class notes was so great that one student, emphasizing their graveness, commented, "We rely so heavily on Masterji's class notes that if he were to stop sharing them, nearly half of us would fail the upcoming semester examination."

Masterji's commitment to assisting his peers and his invaluable contributions to their academic success solidified his position as a respected figure in the college community. His dedication and selflessness made him a source of inspiration and admiration for both students and faculty members.

Despite the girls initially being hesitant to seek help from Masterji or exchange his class notes, they ultimately had no choice but to do so. Masterji, however, had reservations when it came to interacting with girls. There were two primary reasons for this. Firstly, coming from a non-coed small-town school, he had limited exposure to interactions between boys and girls, which were almost forbidden. Secondly, his early experiences with classmates like Rita and her mischievous gang, who had harassed him during his early days in college, left him apprehensive. Whenever the girls approached him, he would instinctively shy away. His reserved behavior, combined with his old-fashioned name, "Manmohan," provided the girls with ammunition to further poke fun at him.

The German department of the college arranged a delightful excursion to a nearby lake city in Haryana. This day-long trip provided the new students with a wonderful opportunity to interact with their classmates, seniors, and esteemed faculty members in a more relaxed and informal setting. Additionally, it offered them a chance to unwind and enjoy themselves outside the confines of the campus.

The trip commenced with a session of introductions, allowing everyone to become acquainted with each other. This was followed by captivating cultural programs that showcased the diverse talents and skills of the students. The atmosphere was filled with joy and enthusiasm as the participants shared their unique performances, creating a sense of camaraderie among the group.

After the cultural festivities, the students were given the freedom to explore and wander around the picturesque lake venue. The serene surroundings, coupled with the refreshing breeze, provided a perfect backdrop for conversations and bonding. Students engaged in animated discussions, sharing their experiences, aspirations, and even their favorite aspects of the German language and culture.

Many students, seeking adventure and amusement, opted for thrilling bike rides, scenic elephant rides, or the unique experience of camel rides. Some preferred a leisurely stroll, relishing the tranquil ambiance of the surroundings. While this was happening, a group of students, including Rita and her companions, chose to set out on a boating adventure. Masterji decided to follow Rita and her friends.

While rowing through the tranquil lake, Masterji could not help but be entranced by the breathtaking allure of the remote, densely wooded area they cruised alongside. Overcome by a surge of emotion and a desire to convey his feelings through music, Masterji found himself unable to resist the impulse. He began to carol the soulful song *"Chhup Chhup Karke..."* concealing himself among the foliage. His melodious voice carried across the tranquil surroundings, creating an atmosphere of serene bliss.

CHHUP CHHUP KARKE
(*Voice*: Mr. Amit Kumar)

Chhup chhup karke dekhun tumhe chup chup karke pyar hua

chhup chhup karke dekhun tumhe chup chup karke pyar hua
pehli nazar me dekha tujhe dil mera kaayal hua… hai
dil mera kaayal hua

Kaatil hai naina chaal sarara kar gaya ghayal yahan
dil ko kar gaya ghayal yahan
ho… tere hi aage chhor diye sab bolo ab jayen kahan… hai
bolo ab jayen kahan
aisi lagan kiya hoke magan kiya dil hi dil me yahan….hoy
tum hi dil me yahan

Chhup chhup karke dekhun tumhe chup chup karke pyar hua
pehli nazar me dekha tujhe dil mera kaayal hua… hai
dil mera kaayal hua

Teri adayen mujhko lubhayein teri wafaon ka sahara
dil ko teri wafaon ka sahara
ho… tujh par hi ab jaan hum denge hai yahi apna irada... hai
hai yahi apna irada
dil to hai pagal aaya tumhi par ab to sambhalo yahon… hoy
tum hi sambhalo yahan

Chhup chhup karke dekhun tumhe chup chup karke pyar hua
pehli nazar me dekha tujhe dil mera kaayal hua… hai
dil mera kaayal hua

Unbeknownst to Masterji, Rita's friends surreptitiously trailed behind him as he passionately sang his heart out. Witnessing this heartfelt performance, they could not help but speculate that his song was dedicated to Rita. Intrigued by this possibility, they began to playfully tease Rita about Masterji's apparent attraction toward her.

With each teasing remark, Rita would swiftly react, her voice filled with a mix of annoyance and defiance. Unwilling to entertain their assumptions, she would assertively shout at her friends, demanding that they cease their playful banter. Rita's commanding presence and her influential background compelled her friends to comply with her wishes.

Aware of the sway Rita held over her friends, she would occasionally shower them with financial gestures, ensuring their loyalty and allegiance. This financial support solidified the bond between Rita and her friends, as they dutifully followed her lead and respected her directives.

As her friends playfully teased her, Rita maintained a composed demeanor, guarding her emotions from their jests. Nevertheless, deep inside, the resonance of Masterji's song and the unspoken sentiments it conveyed left a lasting mark on Rita, sparking her curiosity and kindling her interest in him.

As the weeks went by, the girls astutely observed Masterji's persistent gaze and undeniable attraction to Rita. While the classroom lectures grew increasingly challenging, Masterji's academic prowess continued to earn him praise from the professors. The girls could not help but feel a pang of envy as they witnessed the boys extol Masterji's intelligence, helpfulness, and generosity, all thanks to his comprehensive class notes that simplified their academic lives.

Aware that the boys were leveraging Masterji's notes to gain an edge in their class assignments, the girls found themselves falling behind. A turning point occurred when the girls were humiliated by a professor who informed them that their class assignment rankings were plummeting. The professor warned them that if the situation persisted, they would fail the examination collectively. Feeling embarrassed and worried, the girls decided to devise a plan to entice Masterji into sharing his class notes, as they believed the boys were reaping all the benefits and accolades.

The girls, fully aware of Masterji's fondness for Rita, conspired a plan that would make it seem like Rita reciprocated his feelings. To further their plan, one of their male friends purposefully scoffed Masterji about his affection for Rita in front of their classmates, giving the girls an opening to intensify his interest.

One day, while Masterji and his friend were enjoying their time at a corner tea stall, fate intervened as Rita and her friend coincidentally made a stop at the same stall and unexpectedly joined them. The sudden convergence of their paths surprised both Masterji and his friend, but they warmly cherished the unplanned encounter. Displaying his innate graciousness, Masterji, in his role as a congenial host, promptly ordered tea for their newly arrived guests.

During their conversation, Rita suggested having a private conversation with Masterji, which immediately swept him off his feet. Being unfamiliar with one-on-one conversations with girls, he politely proposed continuing the conversation in the presence of their friends. However, Rita appeared hesitant about discussing the matter openly. Sensing Masterji's reluctance, she decided to proceed with the conversation in front of their friends. With a hint of intrigue in her voice, she asked, "How do you feel about the ongoing rumor about you and me?"

Masterji was taken aback by Rita's mention of the rumor, and he responded with genuine surprise, "I have no idea what you are talking about." His sincerity was evident as he genuinely had no knowledge of any such rumor.

Undeterred, Rita persisted, expressing her admiration for him and suggesting, "I know you are a nice guy. I like you and can be your girlfriend if you want!"

This direct proposal in front of their friends caught Masterji unawares. His village upbringing and cultural values made him astonished that a girl from a wealthy background would openly express her interest in him. Feeling hesitant, he shared his viewpoint, "I do not believe in terms like 'girlfriend' or 'boyfriend'."

Masterji took a moment to gaze at the passing vehicles before resuming, "In my culture, our parents are the ones who determine our future through arranged marriages. Love develops after marriage."

Rita felt offended by his statement. Despite her and her friends' attempts to clarify that she meant their relationship to be purely platonic, Masterji remained steadfast in his belief. He expressed his preference for direct love, rather than engaging in the semantics of labels like "boyfriend" and "girlfriend," and only after successfully crossing that stage, transitioned into love.

This difference of opinion led to a heated argument between them, with neither willing to yield. Masterji eventually grew weary and requested that the ladies leave. However, the girls persistently made efforts to convince him of their genuine desire for a strictly platonic friendship, as they had a hidden agenda of obtaining his class notes.

Eventually, Masterji reached a point of frustration and expressed his decision to discontinue their interaction due to their forceful attitude. As the girls left, they placed the blame on him, perceiving his response as rudeness.

Masterji remained greatly disturbed over the weekend, recognizing that he had unintentionally wounded the sentiments of a girl he held feelings for. His friend attempted to comfort him by explaining that it is unlikely for a girl to reciprocate his love without first getting to know him better. He emphasized that crushes, likes, and friendships are stepping stones that pave the way to the ultimate destination of love.

Masterji realized the mistake he made in hurting Rita's feelings. As the morning class session commenced, he observed that both Rita and her friend seemed upset with him, which further deepened his sense of guilt.

Following the class, Masterji noticed Rita and her friend sitting in front of the library. He mustered up the courage to approach them and asked if he could speak with Rita privately. However, Rita replied with a firm statement, saying, "It is all over now, and I do not want to talk to you."

Masterji grew restless as Rita refused to engage in conversation with him. He pleaded with her, saying, "I will forget you, but please give me a chance to apologize and talk at least."

Rita found herself surprised by Masterji's continued pursuit, displaying behavior that resembled that of someone deeply infatuated. She shared a meaningful glance with her friend, acknowledging that their plan to draw him in was indeed yielding results. Although initially disinterested in taking things any further, Rita eventually conceded to engage in a brief conversation, albeit with strict limitations imposed.

Masterji dared to bite the bullet and started speaking. He expressed his deep admiration for Rita and offered a heartfelt apology for his past actions. Masterji acknowledged that he had made mistakes and clarified that his actions were driven by his genuine feelings for her. With utmost honesty, he expressed his desire to establish a strong and genuine friendship between them.

As Masterji spoke, the girls, including Rita, realized that their mission had been accomplished. Rita, in turn, reciprocated Masterji's sentiments, recognizing the sincerity in his words. The two of them finally reconciled, putting their previous misunderstandings behind them.

With their newfound understanding, Rita became the first person in their class to gain access to Masterji's class notes. However, instead of using this advantage to empower and benefit the entire class, Rita's intentions took a different turn. She began to manipulate Masterji, using his class notes as a means to control and exert authority over their classmates. Through her manipulation, she ensured that everyone had to depend on her for access to the valuable notes.

Rita selectively penalized certain classmates, particularly the boys who had previously been benefiting from Masterji's knowledge. By leveraging her control over the class notes, she established a dominance where others had to seek her favor to obtain valuable information. This allowed her to assert dominance and influence over both Masterji and his classmates.

The situation became worrisome when Rita's behavior shifted to favoring power dynamics and unfair advantages instead of creating an inclusive learning environment. By manipulating Masterji's knowledge, she upset the class balance and made students dependent on her for study materials.

10. Masterji's College Life and Love Story

Masterji had a routine life at JNU, and it was not uncommon for his male classmates to approach him with grievances about the girls, particularly Rita. They claimed that Rita was manipulating Masterji for her benefit, seeking his assistance with college assignments and other tasks. However, Masterji remained oblivious to the truth behind their accusations. He believed that the boys were merely envious of his closeness to the girls, as the girls did not reciprocate the same level of closeness with other male classmates. The boys had grown accustomed to relying on Masterji's assistance, but he was unaware that the girls were not sharing essential class assignments and notes with the boys.

Masterji often found himself teased by his male classmates, who accused him of being a puppet of the girls, especially Rita. Despite the derogatory remarks hurled at him by his dear classmates, Masterji never allowed them to affect him. He endeavored to maintain cordial relationships with all his male and female classmates, demonstrating kindness toward underprivileged boys, a practice that Rita consistently opposed. Rita expressed her displeasure by refusing to communicate with Masterji. As a consequence, Masterji felt compelled to cease helping the male students, as Rita had full control over whom he assisted and whom he did not.

In Masterji's hostel, a fellow student named Sandeep Lamba, who was also from the Jat community and studying Russian, noticed that Masterji was always surrounded by female students in the college. Intrigued by Masterji's popularity with the opposite sex, Lamba's curiosity grew when he discovered that one of the girls, an attractive student named Rita, shared the same Jat background based on her surname. This piqued Lamba's interest even further, leading him to dig deeper and gather more information about her. Through his resourcefulness, Lamba managed to obtain personal details about

Rita, including her background and home address, from the admission department's files. Being from the same Jat community, Lamba felt a sense of familiarity with Rita and saw a potential opportunity to establish a connection with her.

At times, Lamba tried to develop a friendly relationship with Masterji. However, Masterji did not appreciate Lamba's rude rural Haryanvi Jat accent, so he avoided him most of the time. Furthermore, Masterji began to realize that Lamba's attempts to befriend him were motivated by his desire to get closer to Rita, as they both were from the same community.

Lamba made several attempts to approach Rita and introduce himself by his surname, hoping to create a favorable impression by highlighting their shared Jat community. However, Rita did not appreciate Lamba's erratic attitude whenever he tried to approach her. At times, she would taunt him within her group of friends, joking about his name being 'Lamba' despite his short stature. Lamba was under five feet tall, while Rita stood at about five and a half feet tall. Lamba took such sarcasm to his heart.

Whenever Lamba spotted Rita in an isolated area or in the presence of Masterji, he would discreetly tail her, lingering nearby to gaze at her or eavesdrop on her conversations. This persistent intrusion into their private moments started to grate on both Rita and Masterji, causing them annoyance and frustration. Masterji, being well aware of Lamba's impoliteness, made a conscious decision to circumvent engaging with him. After all, Lamba was known to have associations with local troublemakers in town, and Masterji preferred not to get entangled in any unfavorable situations.

However, Lamba's behavior began to unsettle Masterji. At times, he realized that Lamba's approach toward Rita had the potential to jeopardize their relationship. Lamba's looming presence cast a figurative shadow over their interactions, injecting an element of unease and tension into their time together. Masterji's awareness of the negative influence Lamba exerted led him to be cautious of his actions.

Recognizing the implications of Lamba's rude conduct, Masterji grew increasingly concerned that it could strain his bond with Rita. He occasionally contemplated the possibility of losing Rita due to

Lamba's inappropriate behavior. The "Lamba factor" hungover every occasion where Masterji found himself with Rita, subtly affecting their relationship and introducing an undercurrent of tension.

One day, the situation escalated when Rita made a distressing discovery - Lamba had followed her to her home and loitered outside for an extended period. This incident left her feeling deeply frightened and concerned for her safety. The following day, Rita confided in Masterji about Lamba's alarming behavior, seeking his advice. In response, Masterji recommended that she stay cautious and alter her bus timings to avoid Lamba's persistent surveillance. Despite her efforts, however, she still found him lingering near her house on occasion.

As days went by, Masterji's irritation toward Lamba's misconduct grew more pronounced. He wrestled with conflicting emotions, contemplating how best to address the situation without resorting to violence. While he firmly believed in maintaining peace, the internal conflict within him intensified. Some of Masterji's close friends suggested confronting Lamba publicly and using force to teach him a lesson. Their idea was to demonstrate to Lamba, in front of everyone, that he should mind his own business and refrain from interfering in the personal lives of others.

Even in his dreams, Masterji could not escape thoughts of how to rid himself and Rita of Lamba's presence. He frequently imagined taking drastic measures, envisioning himself publicly confronting Lamba at the main campus gathering spot, where a multitude of students congregated. In these dreams, Masterji pictured Lamba pleading for forgiveness, clutching his shins, and making solemn promises to never follow him or Rita again.

Rita, a resourceful and opportunistic individual, dedicated considerable thought to finding a resolution to the Lamba situation. She undertook thorough contemplation, weighing her choices, and was determined not to bring her family into the matter. Rita was aware that escalating the issue might exacerbate future problems. She also acknowledged the possibility of the boys in the hostel sympathizing with Lamba, which could complicate the situation further and pose additional challenges for her.

With her shrewdness, she devised a cunning plan to enlist Masterji's help. Rita hoped that by involving him, he would confront Lamba on her behalf, ultimately enabling her to rid herself of the troublesome figure. Her trickery thinking nature served as her guiding principle as she strategically handled the situation to her advantage.

One fine Sunday morning, Rita sought out Masterji and requested to meet him in an isolated location for a conversation. Intrigued, Masterji accompanied her, unsure of what awaited him. The college campus was devoid of its usual hustle and bustle, as the ongoing vacation had left it deserted and quiet.

To Masterji's surprise, Rita's behavior took an abrupt turn as they settled into their secluded spot. She began showering him with praise and admiration, catching him on the hop with her sudden display of affection. Masterji felt both excited and perplexed, trying to comprehend the reasons behind this unexpected change.

As the conversation progressed, Rita directly posed questions to him, "How much do you like or love me? Do you care for me?"

Masterji was taken aback by the unexpected questions, leaving him feeling startled. He found himself lost and unprepared, uncertain of how to formulate a response. The weight of the moment hung in the air as he grappled with his thoughts.

After a brief pause, Rita repeated the same question, emphasizing her desire for an instant and straightforward answer. The pressure mounted, and Masterji felt the need to provide a response that would satisfy her expectations. However, his mind raced to find the right words to convey his feelings at that moment.

Masterji attempted to seek cover behind an excuse that he was not expecting such sudden questions. However, Rita remained persistent, insisting on receiving his feedback immediately. He hesitated for a moment before responding, "You are very beautiful, and I am attracted to you."

However, Rita was not satisfied with his answer and instantly retorted, "That's it? I constantly hear these words from others, but what is it about you that could truly impress me?" Her taunting words challenged Masterji to dig deeper and prove himself in her eyes.

Masterji was surprised as he was unable to digest her aggressive conversation. So, he tried to deflect her attention on some other issues. However, Rita persisted with the same question. Eventually, Masterji responded, saying, "Yes, I liked you a lot. If given the chance, it could be more than that, perhaps I am in love."

That was all she wanted to know, so that she could proceed with her next plan. Now that she had her mission in place, she began with her agenda, saying, "Do you know my family background? My parents are wealthy and conservative."

She continued with her full story. Masterji was listening with curiosity.

"You know, we Jats are very particular. In my community, girls are married at a young age."

She took a sip of water and proceeded, "However, my parents have decided not to consider any marriage proposals for me before my twenty-sixth birthday. This gives you enough time to achieve success and establish yourself. I hope that you will become a successful individual before that deadline, so that I can introduce you to my family as my chosen groom."

Masterji experienced a range of emotions. While he was delighted by her proactive approach to planning their future as life partners, he could not help but feel baffled about the conditions she was putting forth.

She continued, "Our family holds a high status in society, and my parents have an expectation of marrying me to a civil servant. Can you make a promise to me that you will strive to compete in India's toughest civil service examination? If you succeed, I can then introduce you to my family."

Masterji's gaze remained fixed on the ground as he absorbed her expectations and conditions. Sensing the seriousness of the situation, she bent, drawing closer to him, and looked deeply into his eyes. With a firm tone, she said, "I truly hope you will fulfill this promise. It would bring immense pride to my family to have an Indian Administrative Service (IAS) officer as their son-in-law."

Masterji spoke politely, "Listen, I understand that many students from our university participate in civil service examinations. However, success in these competitions is highly dependent on personal interest and dedication. Furthermore, the outcomes can be unpredictable. I can certainly attempt, but I cannot guarantee anything."

Rita responded firmly, "Yes, but you need to make it more than an attempt. Otherwise, I will consider myself out of your reach." Her irritation with Masterji's response was becoming evident.

Feeling insulted, Masterji tried to get up and leave. However, Rita immediately grabbed his hand, urging him to remain seated. She chirped humbly, "You have exceptional skills in software development, and there are tremendous opportunities in Western countries. My father desires for me to settle in New York, USA. Would you consider pursuing a formal degree to enhance your software expertise and secure a good job in the USA? This way, I can introduce you to my family."

Masterji pondered deeply and finally responded, "Let me carefully consider these options, and I will let you know."

Rita realized that it might be overwhelming for Masterji with all these expectations. In an attempt to evoke his emotions, she moved closer to him and expressed, "I like you a lot and once you fulfill any of these promises, I will fall in love with you."

She was using emotional manipulation and bargaining in the name of love. However, Masterji trusted her words. As a gesture of appreciation, she offered him tickets to a matinee movie show at Priya Cinema, Vasant Vihar. During the show, their conversation shifted to her hidden agenda concerning Lamba. Rita disclosed, "You are aware that Lamba constantly follows us. He even followed me to my home and sometimes he stayed outside of my house for several hours."

Masterji listened attentively, patiently taking in the information.

"I came to know that Lamba's family is politically influential and wealthy. Furthermore, he is from my community. If he approached my father about me, my father would surrender me to him."

Finally, she requested Masterji, "Please do something for Lamba, otherwise you might lose me to him."

She directly pitched Masterji against Lamba.

The college election was approaching, and a student from Korean studies was running for the position of Vice President (VP) in the college's Student Union. He learned that Masterji was very popular among students in the German Department, which had the highest enrollment. Therefore, he sought Masterji's support to maximize his votes from the department.

Masterji was sitting with his hostel mates in his room. They were frolicking when the VP candidate appeared at the door. He came to Masterji's room to urge for his support in the election. The VP candidate was desperate for votes, and he was hoping that Masterji and his friends could help him.

The VP candidate was persuasive, and his requests seemed to appeal to Masterji and his friends. However, as they were discussing their support for him, one of Masterji's colleagues pointed out that his ex-roommate, who lived next door, was from the Spanish Department and was very popular. He suggested that the VP candidate should approach him to get more votes from the Spanish Department.

The ex-roommate agreed to support the VP candidate, but he put forward a condition. If the VP candidate won the election, he would have to bring a 750 mL bottle of Chivas Regal 25-year-old blended, single malt Scotch Whisky each for both Masterji and himself on the night of the election for his victory celebration. The VP candidate accepted his proposal, and Masterji and his friends blessed him in advance that only he would win the election. This was a substantial endorsement for the candidate, as Masterji was a respected and influential figure among the students.

Once the VP candidate left the room, Masterji jokingly said to his friends, "Pals, I just occasionally take one or two sips of whiskey with you guys, but I am not as fond of alcohol as you all are."

His friends shrieked with laughter, and one of them asked incredulously, "What? You have never tasted alcohol before college?"

Masterji nodded with a smile. "That is correct. You and your friends are the only ones who have given me a taste of it from time to time. Otherwise, I am not particularly fond of it."

The friends continued to crack jokes, and one of them teased, "Do not worry, you will have more opportunities to drink alcohol in a day or two."

Masterji shook his head and said, "No, thank you. I actually find it unpleasant, especially beer. It smells like urine to me."

This caused the friends to split into sides again, some laughing while others groaned in disgust. Masterji quickly added, "Sorry, friends! Not to offend you, but that's just my opinion."

As the friends dispersed, they punned about how they hoped the VP candidate would lose so they would not have to provide the promised bottle of whiskey. Masterji chimed in, "I too hope he loses."

But his ex-roommate reminded him, "How can he lose when both of us have endorsed him?"

The friends giggled and agreed that they were all looking forward to a free drink and a party the next night. Finally, they all dispersed.

During the day of the election, Masterji's hostel mates reminded him and his ex-roommate of the promise they had made to support the VP candidate. Reminded of honoring their commitment, they jointly assumed the responsibility of promoting the VP candidate in their respective academic departments, where the highest voter turnout was anticipated. Leveraging their charisma and eloquence, they passionately persuaded their fellow students to support the VP candidate, emphasizing his strengths and leadership attributes. They also addressed any apprehensions or reservations their peers had regarding the candidate's suitability for the position.

Their tireless dedication bore fruit. The VP candidate secured a substantial number of votes from both academic departments, culminating in his resounding victory in the election. This accomplishment marked a momentous victory, not only for the VP candidate but also for Masterji and his former roommate. Their support proved instrumental in securing the candidate's success, showcasing their loyalty and commitment to their word, despite the numerous roadblocks.

Following his victory in the college student union election, the VP candidate fulfilled his promise by arriving in the evening with the two whiskey bottles as a token of gratitude. However, as word spread about the victory and the presence of whiskey, other hostel mates gathered and demanded a celebratory party, with some requesting additional whiskey bottles. So, before saying goodbye, he ordered additional bottles and cocktail snacks for the jubilant hostel mates of Masterji.

They gathered for the party, but Masterji's ex-roommate and other hostel mates had different plans. Some of these friends were offended by Masterji's comment about comparing beer to urine and decided to rag on him. They wanted to make him drink like a fish and play a prank on him as he was new to their group. Without informing Masterji, they made a bet to see how much alcohol it would take to make him drunk, looking forward to the possible scene created by his intoxication.

During the party, one colleague announced, "We are having a bet that whoever drinks the maximum amount of neat whiskey will be declared a superhero in the hostel."

Masterji initially tried to avoid the bet, but his friends challenged him, and he eventually accepted the challenge. Unbeknownst to Masterji, his friends cleverly started serving him the maximum amount of neat whiskey, while the others were either secretly drinking diluted whiskey or throwing away their pegs in the dark. As a result, Masterji consumed almost a full bottle of neat whiskey in a short time.

As the evening ripened, the excessive alcohol consumption began to take its toll on Masterji, leading to severe nausea and vomiting. His friends helped him clean up and then isolated him in his room. Masterji, in his intoxicated state, fell asleep and had a disturbing dream about Lamba, who often followed Rita when she was alone or with him.

Masterji's dream was deeply unsettling. It brought to the forefront his fear of Lamba's behavior and the conversation he had with Rita about her father possibly agreeing to her marriage with Lamba through their community connections. Masterji also witnessed Lamba successfully winning her parents' confidence, with both Rita and Lamba agreeing to the marriage. Suddenly awakened from this bad dream, Masterji grabbed a hockey stick and rushed to find Lamba, whose room was located downstairs.

Lamba's loyal friends alerted him to go into hiding, as Masterji was on the lookout for him. They informed him that Masterji was armed with a hockey stick, seeking to settle the score for Lamba's actions during their college session. Although Masterji managed to reach Lamba's room, his drunken state caused him to stumble and lose consciousness again. Meanwhile, Lamba had stealthily absconded through a rear exit, finding refuge in an undisclosed location.

Masterji's friends, faced with the daunting task of managing his intoxicated escapades, mustered great effort to extract him from Lamba's room and transport him back to the safety of his own quarters. Throughout the night, Masterji repeatedly attempted to resume his search for Lamba, driven by a mix of anger and a desire for retribution.

Each time, his friends intercepted him, forcibly steering him away from his futile mission. The loop of pursuit and intervention persisted throughout the night, until Masterji's friends eventually decided to lock him inside his room, providing him respite from his fruitless endeavors.

At the same time, Lamba's friends, cognizant of the escalating tension and the possible repercussions of his actions, recommended that he temporarily vacate the hostel. Understanding the graveness of the situation and fearing the wrath of Masterji and his friends, Lamba reluctantly followed their counsel. He opted for a few days of seclusion, away from the hostel environment.

Upon learning that Lamba had taken a temporary leave from the hostel, Masterji's friends informed him of the situation, advising him not to hastily pursue Lamba. Severely intoxicated and still healing from the effects of the excessive whiskey consumption, Masterji acknowledged the need to cede control to his friends for the following few days.

In the rare moments of clarity amidst his intoxication, Masterji's sole focus remained on seeking revenge against Lamba. His motivation did not only come from personal reasons but also from the information shared by his girlfriend, Rita. She had disclosed Lamba's unwelcomed advances and his persistent habit of following her, even to her house. Rita had expressed her desire for Masterji to confront Lamba and teach him a lesson that would dissuade him from continuing his intrusive behavior.

Throughout the college, whispers of Masterji's pursuit of Lamba ran wild. The absence of the formidable Lamba only added to the anticipation and curiosity among their peers. Rita, buoyed by the belief that Masterji was seeking vengeance on her behalf, found herself elated by the prospect.

However, Lamba's friends, cognizant of the potential consequences of an altercation with Masterji and his companions, urged Lamba to reconcile and make peace. They emphasized that Masterji, being equally strong and supported by friends who surpassed Lamba and his allies in physical prowess, posed a substantial threat. The possibility of Lamba suffering a humiliating defeat in such a confrontation was evident.

Taking their advice to heart, Lamba approached Rita with a rakhi, symbolizing a sacred bond between siblings. In a jaw-dropping twist, Lamba proposed that Rita accept him as her brother. In return, Rita tied a rakhi on Lamba's wrist, signifying their newfound sibling relationship. This gesture fulfilled Rita's underlying motive, providing her with a sense of security and protection.

The news of the reconciliation between Lamba and Rita reached Masterji through Rita herself. She expressed her gratitude to him for compelling Lamba to seek peace and accepting her as his sister. Masterji found solace in the fact that his efforts had led to the resolution of the Lamba situation. This, in turn, brought Rita closer to him and strengthened the trust in their relationship. While some classmates remained skeptical of Rita's intentions and perceived selfishness in her closeness to Masterji, they still congratulated him for resolving the issue with Lamba.

For Masterji, several benefits emerged from this chain of events. Firstly, the Lamba factor had been resolved, alleviating the immediate threat and discomfort. Secondly, Rita's newfound trust and closeness to him instilled a deeper connection in their relationship. Lastly, because of his severe health condition caused by excessive drinking, Masterji made the firm decision to abstain from alcohol altogether.

With a sense of accomplishment and a newfound determination to prioritize his well-being, Masterji embarked on a path that would not only shape his personal growth but also solidify his bond with Rita, while leaving the turbulence surrounding Lamba behind.

Masterji's classmates, especially the trusted female friends, were giving him negative impressions of Rita. They were warning him that Rita had no affection for him. Instead, she was just using him for her benefit, such as his help with the class assignments. Masterji did not realize those female friends were actually his well-wishers as they cared about him. They were trying to save him from Rita's selfish trap.

Masterji did not trust the words of his classmates. In fact, he taunted the girls that they were just jealous of his closeness with Rita. He further told them that because of Rita he was not giving any weightage to them and that was why they were trying to sully his friendship with Rita.

One day it reached a climax when a couple of his female friends saw him in the company of Rita. She just went to the restroom while Masterji was waiting outside. One friend shouted at him, saying, "Oye, sycophant, do not forget us."

The second friend politely alerted him, "Dear friend, beware of her selfishness and stay away from her, otherwise you will spoil your life because of this toxic girl."

Masterji experienced a sense of insult due to the continuous derogatory remarks from his female friends. He could not comprehend why they were criticizing Rita and his friendship with her as he did not perceive anything wrong with Rita's behavior toward him. Unable to tolerate it any longer, he made up his mind to have an open and honest conversation with the girls.

He found his trusted friends at the food court and joined them. One of the ladies commented, "You are alone today. Where is your goddess?"

Masterji thought that was a perfect time to clarify things with them. He informed the friends that Rita herself had approached him several times in the past. She was also his well-wisher like any other female classmate, and she was not using him for her purpose. In fact, Rita was a nice person. Finally, he told them how she had recently come to meet him on Sunday. She accompanied him to a movie and confessed that she was in love. On that day, she came with a marriage proposal to marry him after her twenty-sixth birthday. Masterji further narrated how she wanted to settle with him in the United States of America.

The girls gossiped about how Rita was befooling him. They could not believe Rita's bluff to Masterji. The girls felt sorry for Masterji for trusting Rita and suspected that she might have ulterior motives for misleading him. In an attempt to reveal the truth, they decided to verify Masterji's conversation with Rita.

During a class break, the girls spotted Rita and Masterji sitting outside the library. They playfully teased Rita about her movie and proposal to Masterji. Eventually, the girls confronted Rita, urging her to clarify the truth about Masterji's conversations with them. Without hesitation, Rita denied everything that Masterji had said, even swearing her father's name to emphasize her denial.

Masterji was taken aback by Rita's rebuttal. It was the first time he doubted her credibility and honesty. He wondered if there might be a hidden reason behind her refusal. Despite his doubts, he still loved her deeply and chose to believe that there might be some valid explanation for her actions. He did not confront her or challenge her claims because his love for her compelled him to give her the benefit of the doubt. Masterji did not feel it was appropriate to cross-verify the information he had heard. In his mind, he considered that he may have misunderstood or misinterpreted the situation. On the other hand, Masterji's female friends trusted him. They knew Rita's character well and were not surprised by her attempts to deceive or bluff.

After Masterji inadvertently disclosed a personal conversation with Rita, which she vehemently denied in front of their classmates, she grew irritated with him for revealing their private discussion. Without offering any explanation, she stopped talking to him and began boycotting him.

Masterji felt a sense of disappointment and insult as Rita ignored him. The classmates, observing the sudden change in their dynamic, seized the opportunity to take a dig at Masterji, reveling in his exclusion. Although this phase was painful for Masterji, he had become somewhat accustomed to enduring such emotional turmoil, as Rita had often taken advantage of his kindness in the past, only to later sideline him.

Nonetheless, Masterji chose to take the situation lightly, holding onto the hope that Rita would eventually come back seeking his help and favor, as she had done countless times before. Moreover, he found solace in the fact that the approaching final year exams would likely bring her back to him, as she would require his support once again. True to his expectations, Rita eventually reciprocated, showing friendship, affection, love, and respect to Masterji, all to secure his favor.

Their classmates, having witnessed this pattern between Masterji and Rita in the past, were not overly surprised by the truce between the compassionate Masterji and the cunning Rita. It seemed to be a familiar cycle playing out once again, with both parties resuming their previous roles.

While there was an underlying skepticism, Masterji maintained his composure and refrained from displaying any negative emotions toward Rita. He understood the value of being supportive and helpful, even if he was doubtful about her true intentions. Thus, he extended his usual assistance to her without letting his reservations affect their interactions.

Masterji's approach demonstrated his maturity and ability to navigate complex relationships. Despite his doubts, he chose not to let them overshadow his commitment to kindness and support. Deep down, he hoped that his caution would prove to be unwarranted and that Rita would eventually prove herself trustworthy.

11. Love's Trials: Masterji & Rita

After the final exams and the declaration of results, all the students gathered to bid farewell to each other as they prepared to take the next steps in their careers. Many students who achieved first-class results were planning to pursue a master's degree in the university's postgraduate department. Some had made other commitments and chosen different paths. Masterji, having topped the exams, had his sights set on the master's program in the university's postgraduate department, as he had always planned.

Rita, too, had an interest in the master's program, but she missed qualifying for admission by just a few marks, falling short of the first-class requirement. However, there was still hope as she had submitted a request for re-evaluation of her last exam, hoping to make the grade.

After the students exchanged farewells, they dispersed. Rita approached Masterji and requested his company to the university's special bus stop. Masterji obliged and accompanied her to the stop, but unfortunately, she missed the bus. Faced with this situation, she hired an autorickshaw and asked Masterji to join her till the road to her house.

In the autorickshaw, she displayed frustration and accused Masterji of being selfish. Rita believed that Masterji had topped the exam but failed to guide her properly to achieve the desired first-class marks.

So, she felt that she would not qualify for admission to the master's program she was desperately interested in. She leveled multiple accusations against Masterji, asserting that he placed his studies above all else, which left her feeling unsettled and misled. In her view, his friendship, love, affection, and emotions had been detrimental, hindering her ability to concentrate on her studies.

Masterji was deeply hurt by her statements and allegations, as he was genuinely devoted to helping her. In fact, he had hoped that she would achieve better grades than him. However, Masterji chose not to express any displeasure over her accusations because he realized that it might be their final meeting.

As the autorickshaw approached a bus stop near her home, she decided to disembark. She intentionally got off a few blocks away from her house to ensure that no one in her neighborhood would discover that she was accompanied by a boy.

Masterji was once again hurt because he knew this would be their final meeting. She did not even invite him to her home, which was just a few blocks away, to introduce him to her parents as a fellow student. Furthermore, she abruptly exited the autorickshaw while catapulting numerous blame at him.

For a while, Masterji was disturbed by the unjustified accusations that he was the reason for her lack of success. He pondered over how he could regain her trust and convince her to attend the master's program she desired, to make her happy. Despite having some issues with her attitude, he still loved her genuinely and wished to be in her company during the master's program.

One day, Masterji came across a new announcement from the university stating that if any confirmed applicants dropped out, candidates who obtained marks below first class would have a chance to secure admission. As the application deadline approached, Masterji realized he should inform Rita about this opportunity. However, he could not forget how she had mistreated and annoyed him during their last encounter in the autorickshaw. This made him hesitant and fearful about contacting her directly.

Masterji sought the help of a close female classmate, a trusted friend, to deliver an admission application form to Rita's home. He aimed to persuade Rita to complete the form as per the university's recent announcement, which would improve her chances of admission. Masterji specifically instructed his friend not to reveal that he was the one behind the delivery.

At first, the female friend warned Masterji about his concern for Rita, given the insults, allegations, and annoyances she had directed at him previously. Masterji admired his lovely friend, but he informed her that he loved Rita deeply and was willing to do anything to make her happy. The friend reciprocated his admiration for Rita but made it clear and vocalized that she had great respect for him and enjoyed his smiling face. However, she expressed her fear of losing the smile of her friend because of Rita's past actions, suggesting that Rita might hurt him in the future.

She cautioned him that Rita was nothing more than a dirt stain on a white shirt, just as she was on Masterji's heart. She emphasized the importance of being cautious and removing such dirt stains promptly before they have a chance to stick to the skin and cause any kind of harm. Masterji acknowledged her advice and teasingly asked if she was jealous of Rita. He further taunted her, saying, "Are you eagerly waiting for the day when Rita is out of the picture, so you can try your luck with me?"

She laughed and clarified, "It is not just me, but many girls are interested in you. However, my concern lies elsewhere. I simply want you to avoid falling into the wrong hands or becoming entangled in a deceptive trap."

Masterji tried to playfully provoke her, saying, "That's all?"

She responded, "Please do not interpret my words in any other way. If you wish, I will be your best friend."

Masterji happily agreed, saying, "Yes, indeed! Thank you."

Finally, she assured him, "I will follow your instructions and visit Rita's house to persuade her to apply for the master's program."

Rita's family members discovered that she had received an application form for a master's program from a classmate who had recently visited her home. However, her parents strongly opposed her decision to pursue a master's degree. They thought it would be more beneficial for Rita to gain practical experience or undergo specific coaching. That would endow her with the knowledge needed to contribute to their diverse family business. Their specific preference was for her to manage the media branch of the family business. As a result, Rita had to abandon her plans to pursue a master's degree.

When the master classes commenced, one day Rita unexpectedly appeared at the department in search of Masterji. After some searching, she finally found him, and they engaged in a lengthy discussion. Rita was curious to know why Masterji had sent a female classmate to her house with the master's application form, attempting to persuade her to submit the application.

Initially, Masterji denied the notion that he had sent a girl to Rita's house and insisted there was no ulterior motive. However, Rita believed that Masterji still nestled feelings for her and that was the main reason behind sending the application form, hoping she would stay with him.

Their conversation took a teasing tone, with Rita questioning why girls were so sympathetic toward Masterji and always willing to go to great lengths for him. Masterji replied with a witty one-liner, stating that the girls were his true friends. Rita then questioned what her position was in his life. Eventually, she alleged that Masterji had a connection with the girl he had sent to her house and suggested he should pursue that relationship instead.

In the midst of their conversation, Masterji unintentionally hurt Rita's feelings by remarking, "It always happens when someone goes to a new place; new friendships begin, and memories of the old place and old friends fade away."

This comment deeply hurt Rita, and her anger became evident on her face. Despite Masterji's attempts to calm and persuade her to stay and not take it too seriously, she left the place in a fit of anger. Masterji felt insulted.

After several weeks, a mutual friend informed Masterji that Rita had enrolled in a nearby coaching institute for mass media training. Masterji felt both joyful and apprehensive at the news. He was thrilled at the prospect of seeing her again, but he could not shake off the memory of their last meeting when she abruptly left him in the middle of a conversation out of anger.

Masterji wrote a greeting card with apologies and expressed his love for Rita, intending to give it to her when they met. Upon arriving at the coaching institute, he found Rita sitting with other girls, including some of their former classmates. Among them was a particular girl who had always been nasty toward Masterji and seemed to have a close relationship with Rita. This girl consistently shared negative stories about Masterji with Rita, creating tension between them. Unfortunately, Masterji now had to face this unpleasant individual.

After much effort, Rita reluctantly agreed to take Masterji's greeting card. She read it and kept it in her purse. Masterji felt elated that she had accepted his gesture. However, Rita did not invite him to sit or engage in conversation. Instead, she curtly left the institute with an urgent excuse.

A day or two later, when Masterji had some free time, he approached Rita again. However, she was once again in the company of the same repellent girl. Masterji repeatedly requested Rita for a cup of coffee, and finally, she agreed. All three of them went to a coffee shop.

Rita took out Masterji's greeting card and attempted to return it to him, stating, "I am not that type of girl. So, I am returning it to you."

Masterji requested a private conversation with Rita, but she firmly held her friend's hand, insisting that she would not speak to strangers in private, following her mother's advice.

As a result, Rita's friend remained seated and listened to their conversation. Masterji pleaded with Rita to keep the greeting card, clarifying that it was merely an apology and a way to express his feelings. However, in anger, she tore the card into tiny pieces and handed them back to Masterji. She further warned him that she did not want to see any unwanted guests like him again. Rita's behavior was so strange that neither her friend nor Masterji could comprehend it.

Masterji felt completely heartbroken by the insult he had received in front of a third person. In his anguish, he exclaimed, "I know many girls like you are eager to be part of my company and friendship."

Feeling deeply hurt, Masterji left the place in remorse.

He had his semester exams in a couple of days, but Masterji remained deeply disturbed by Rita's attitude and found it difficult to focus on his studies. Intent on apologizing and resolving the situation, he met with her the next day to express his regrets for their previous encounter and the hurtful words he had spoken.

Masterji managed to catch up with Rita and her friend on the staircase of the institute. As he was going up and they were coming down, he sincerely apologized to Rita and asked her to stop and have a conversation. However, she ignored his request and continued walking, deliberately avoiding any interaction. Desperate, Masterji pleaded, "Please listen, I have my exam tomorrow, and for my sake, please just spare a moment. I cannot concentrate on my studies otherwise."

Despite his earnest plea, Rita showed no respect or consideration and walked away. Frustrated, he turned to the other lady, hoping she would intervene and stop Rita. Instead, she taunted him by recalling his earlier statement, "What did you mean by 'many girls like you' the other day?" Both Rita and her friend disregarded his request and left him standing there.

Masterji returned feeling heartbroken, unable to shake off the disappointment of the encounter. His attempt to reconcile and find closure had only resulted in further pain.

The following day, Masterji had a semester exam. Despite his emotional turmoil, he managed to appear for the exam, but his performance was greatly affected, and he felt that the exam was completely spoiled. After completing the exam, as he walked out of the examination hall, he noticed Rita sitting alone under a tree in their department, seemingly waiting for him. However, instead of approaching her, Masterji decided to change his path and disappeared from the scene, choosing not to engage with her.

Masterji had been lost in his thoughts and unable to focus on his studies for days. Eventually, an ex-classmate from their undergraduate days invited Masterji, Rita, and their other friends to celebrate his birthday together. Amidst the gathering, Masterji's friends encouraged him to sing a song for everyone. Initially hesitant, he eventually gave in to their persistent requests and approached the microphone to sing the song "*Muskurahat Me Teri...*"

MUSKURAHAT ME TERI
(*Voice*: Mr. Kumar Sanu)

hun u hun hu hun u hun hu.......hey a ha hey a aa......
Muskurahat me teri koi shararat bhari hai

pyar ki ek jhalak me zindagani basi hai, zindagani basi hai
muskurahat me teri koi shararat bhari hai
pyar ki ek jhalak me zindagani basi hai, zindagani basi hai

Mur ke dekhe na tu
mur ke dekhe na tu, mil ke jaye na tu
aisi koi dil me ab chahat nahi hai
ab chahat nahi hai

Dilruba tu kahin ja
dilruba tu kahin ja, dil kahe tu paas aa
inkar bhi karde koi shikayat nahi hai
koi shikayat nahi hai

Muskurahat me teri koi shararat bhari hai
pyar ki ek jhalak me zindagani basi hai, zindagani basi hai

Tujh se pyar jo kiya hun
tujh se pyar jo kiya hun, bekarar dil kiya hun
ye wafai jafai ab sada sang rahegi
ab sada sang rahegi

Karta hun ye wada
karta hun ye wada, dil ka hai ek irada
intezar mein teri zindagani rahegi
zindagani rahegi…

As Masterji chorused the song, his friends and even Rita interpreted it as a dedication to her. Several girls approached Rita, attempting to convince her that Masterji had genuine and deep feelings of love for her. They spotlighted his handsome appearance, impressive physique, intelligence, and intellect, which made him stand out among their circle of friends. Rita herself felt an attraction toward Masterji, and the song only served to further ignite newfound feelings of love in her heart for him.

In the course of a few days, Masterji decided to quit his studies. The constant feeling of being ignored by Rita greatly affected his ability to concentrate and focus. To distance himself from the place and the memories associated with Rita, he chose to leave his studies behind and move away.

Masterji departed from Delhi and returned to his village, where he decided to assist his grandma in running the local school. Additionally, he decided to pursue software development and engage in community service from his village. Engrossed in his new life, he became deeply involved in various community initiatives and embraced the rural lifestyle, gradually forgetting about the city and its past events.

Despite grandma's persistence about his marriage, Masterji kept postponing the conversation by assuring her that he was not ready yet and would let her know when the time was right. However, he did confide in his dear friend John, a Christian man, about his college love story. John held a special place in Masterji's heart, and they shared a close bond, which allowed Masterji to open up and share his experiences with him.

One day, Masterji received a love letter from Rita, filled with apologies and her confession of missing him. In the letter, Rita expressed her love for Masterji, stating that he meant more to her than anything else. She also informed him that she had already spoken to her parents about him, and they had given their consent for their marriage without any conditions. Rita eagerly invited Masterji to her home to meet her parents as soon as possible, solidifying her commitment to their relationship.

Upon receiving Rita's love letter, Masterji was overjoyed and could not contain his excitement. Receiving the love letter felt like discovering a hidden treasure chest, unlocking the vault of affection with each word on the page. He immediately shared the news with his close friend John, who shared in his happiness and celebrated the development. John, in turn, conveyed the joyful news to Masterji's grandma, seeking her consent on his behalf.

At first, Masterji's grandma became upset that Masterji had not personally informed her about the letter. However, after understanding the situation, she could not help but feel joyous for Masterji. In fact, she was so delighted that she instructed John to book Masterji's railway ticket, facilitating his journey to meet Rita's parents and formally seek their consent for their marriage. The next day, John dropped Masterji to a nearby railway station and from there, Masterji took a train to meet Rita and her family.

12. Tejas Joined the Indian Army-Training

Tejas went for training at the Indian Military Academy, where he encountered a strict and irritating trainer named Pitambar Singh Suryavanshi. Pitambar always boasted about his name, claiming that his parents believed he was a reincarnation of Lord Vishnu himself. He even exaggerated that the priest had discovered all the divine qualities in him at birth, predicting that he would one day become a savior of humanity. That was why they had bestowed upon him the name 'Pitambar.'

However, there was no evidence of any divine characteristics or discipline in him. In fact, he often behaved in a manner completely contrary to godliness. Years ago, the senior trainees at the training school had given him the nickname "Pissu," a shortened version derived from his full name. Whenever he passed by, the trainees would mock him, calling out "Pissu" in jest, which he found quite demeaning. Unfortunately, he had no recourse other than assigning arduous tasks to the trainees.

In response, Pitambar would assign the trainees a series of challenging and physically demanding tasks as a way to assert his authority and teach them discipline. These tasks included grueling long-distance marches, intense endurance training sessions, rigorous combat drills, and punishing physical fitness tests. Additionally, he would make them perform tedious and repetitive tasks, such as cleaning and organizing the training grounds, polishing equipment for hours on end, and maintaining strict discipline in all aspects of their training.

After a week of freshman training, a new recruit joined the training school. Due to his medical condition, he had been delayed in joining. By this time, Tejas had already settled in and established friendships within the new environment. The new recruit was Javed

Khan, a Muslim from J&K, and he quickly earned the nickname "JK" among his peers.

Within just a day or two, JK showcased his exceptional skills and professionalism, surpassing his fellow trainees. His performance in the military training school stood out prominently. However, because of his exceptional abilities, background from J&K, and being a Muslim, both the trainer and many of his colleagues harbored suspicions that he might have a connection to terrorism or prior military training. They speculated that JK could be an agent of a Pakistani terrorist group, sent with malicious intentions to spy on and harm the military training school. Consequently, he became the target of secret criticism, frequent bullying, and occasional harassment by both the trainer and his colleagues.

On numerous occasions, the trainer would nitpick and highlight trivial mistakes made by JK, subjecting him to harsh punishments and assigning him extra grueling workouts. These actions seemed unnecessary and unjust to both JK and some of the other trainees, including Tejas. While many disapproved of the trainer's treatment of JK, no one dared to openly challenge or revolt against the trainer's behavior.

Tejas, however, made attempts to protect JK from the unfair treatment, even though his efforts proved unsuccessful. Despite the lack of success, JK noticed Tejas's genuine concern and support.

One day, Tejas came across JK in a state of deep sadness and tears at a secluded spot. Sensing his distress, Tejas approached JK and offered him consolation. He reassured JK that he was there for him and would stand by him through his difficulties. JK, finding peace in Tejas's presence, poured out his emotions and shared his pain. Tejas, understanding the weight of JK's burden, leaned in and offered his shoulder as a source of comfort.

Through their conversation, JK discovered a true friend in Tejas. He confided in him, explaining that despite being a Muslim from J&K, he was a patriot like everyone else in the training camp. He acknowledged the suspicions his colleagues held due to his background but emphasized that his own family had suffered at the hands of militants. JK revealed his personal history to Tejas and requested that it remain confidential, entrusted only to him.

JK revealed to Tejas a tragic incident from his childhood. When he was around 8 years old, terrorists targeted his home in search of his 16-year-old brother. They demanded that his brother join their organization and be sent to a militant camp in Pakistan-occupied Kashmir (PoK). However, JK's parents stood against this and refused to let their son be a part of such violence.

In a brutal act of retaliation, the terrorists mercilessly killed both of JK's parents and his elder brother. The terrorists then left, searching for another young male to recruit. JK and his sister witnessed this horrifying act while hiding in fear. It was a traumatic experience that left a lasting impact on JK's life.

Before taking her last breath, JK's mother, sensing the imminent danger, made a heartfelt plea to him. She urged JK to escape from the village, pursue his education diligently, serve the nation when he grew up, and be a helping hand to those in need. It was a solemn promise that JK made to his mother, etching those words deep in his heart.

Together with his sister, JK fled to their aunt's home in another village, where they found refuge. His aunt's husband, recognizing the dire circumstances they had faced, adopted JK and his sister and gave them his own surname. In this new environment, JK diligently pursued his education and eventually qualified for military school. His life's purpose was to serve the nation and assist those in need, just as he had promised his mother.

Tejas consistently shielded JK from the trainer and his confrontational colleagues, providing him with protection, assistance, and support. JK grew to regard Tejas as a trusted friend and held him in high esteem. Their friendship blossomed, and they shared a strong bond and camaraderie. Tejas would occasionally refer to JK as "Hey baradar!" and JK would promptly respond with, "Yes baradar!!"

Alongside their fellow trainees, Tejas and JK engaged in various unconventional and enjoyable activities. During one incident, Tejas noticed the trainer bathing in the open air, which sparked a mischievous idea in his mind. For several days, he had been observing a bee's nest on a branch of a tall tree behind his dormitory, which happened to be near the tube-well where the trainer bathed. Armed with a catapult, Tejas began aiming and launching stones at the bee's nest from his dormitory window.

After several unsuccessful attempts, Tejas finally managed to hit the center of the nest. Immediately, a swarm of bees started buzzing toward the origin of the disturbance, searching for the one who had attacked them. Tejas swiftly closed his window, remaining unharmed. The bees continued their chase, and within moments, the entire atmosphere was filled with the presence and buzzing of the bees. Many people sought shelter to avoid the bees' wrath.

Unfortunately, the trainer could not avoid the situation since he was in the middle of taking a bath, without any clothes on, and still covered in soap. Despite his efforts, luck was not on his side. The bees swiftly targeted him as their prey, attracted by his wet and unclothed state. The trainer endured a severe onslaught from the battalion of bees, suffering numerous stings. Thankfully, he was ultimately rescued by others who came to his aid. However, the trainer was left with severe injuries from the bee bites.

After a period of recovery from his injuries, the trainer began an investigation to uncover what had agitated the bees. Through a reliable source, he learned that Tejas was responsible for the incident. Enraged, the trainer hurriedly made his way toward the residence hall in search of Tejas. Word quickly spread among Tejas's colleagues, alerting him to the trainer's intentions. In a state of alarm, Tejas locked his room from the inside. Determined to confront Tejas, the trainer instructed others to force their way through the front door. Upon barging into the room, they discovered that Tejas had already made his escape through the window.

Tejas, with the assistance of his friends, staged an accident and was admitted to the hospital as part of their plan. The news of Tejas's condition reached his colleagues and the trainer, who visited him at the hospital to express their sympathy. Seeing Tejas in a vulnerable state, the trainer was moved and decided to forgive him for the incident with the bees. Unbeknownst to the trainer, he overheard a conversation between Tejas and his friends, revealing the truth behind the accident ruse. However, by that time, the trainer had formed a positive impression of Tejas based on his other commendable actions. Consequently, the trainer chose to overlook and forgive Tejas for his mischievous involvement with the bees.

In another incident, Tejas and JK executed a phone prank on the trainer. The plan originated when they observed the trainer conversing intimately with a lady receptionist who wore a hijab at a hospital. They suspected that the trainer was displaying unusual softness toward her, considering his typically rude and aggressive demeanor. As part of the hospital visit program, the trainer divulged his personal information to the receptionist. Tejas seized this opportunity and proposed a clever idea to JK.

With access to the trainer's personal information, including his phone number and address provided to the receptionist, Tejas and JK took advantage of the trainer's vulnerability toward her. They devised a leg-pull by impersonating the receptionist, Saira Banu, and using her name to tease and harass the trainer. Saira Banu was renowned for her shyness, which was especially notable due to the pronunciation of her name.

The trainer was unable to see her face, but he noticed her hands, feet, and partially uncovered hair, which he found attractive. During their conversation, he asked for her name, and upon learning it, he felt ecstatic, imagining her resemblance to a Bollywood actress from the 70s. In a momentary lapse, he envisioned himself with the actress in a flashback scene set by a mountain lake, accompanied by a popular 70s song. However, his reverie was abruptly interrupted when a patient's wheelchair accidentally bumped into his leg. Despite the interruption, the trainer's infatuation persisted, and he mustered the courage to express his desire to meet her after her duty. He assured her that she could call him anytime, eagerly awaiting her call. Just as the trainer's number was called from the doctor's office, he had to bid the receptionist a warm goodbye, expressing his hope of seeing her again.

The conversation between the trainer and the receptionist gave Tejas and JK a new recipe. One day, Tejas called the trainer during off-hours. He placed a handkerchief on the landline phone receiver and mimicked the voice of the hospital receptionist. At first, Tejas imitated the receptionist's shyness. However, as the conversation became more thrilling for the trainer, Tejas also matched the energy. In the lady's voice, Tejas informed the trainer that she would like to see him clean-shaven without a mustache. The trainer was briefly surprised, as he frequently boasted about his long, thick mustache like military personnel when interacting with the younger trainees, some of whom had little or no mustache. He would usually twist his mustaches with haughtiness to tease the new recruits.

The lady's voice extended an invitation to the trainer, suggesting a meeting at a coffee shop. She explained her family and community's strictness and the dangers that could befall boys from outside if they got involved with their girls, such as stabbings or even death. This made the trainer nervous, but he reassured her by underscoring his martial arts training as an army man, emphasizing that she should be proud of him. He confidently stated that he was not afraid of anyone and claimed to possess the ability to confront a force of a thousand men single-handedly. In response, she proposed wearing a particular hijab and being accompanied by her cousin-sister to avoid suspicion from her family and community members. The trainer agreed to the plan and scheduled a specific time for their meeting.

Tejas executed his plan by bribing a group of hijras. As part of the plan, the freshers were invited to witness a magic show near the coffee shop. Two hijras were dressed in hijab to resemble the receptionist girl and her sister, and they occupied a table in the center of the coffee shop. Additionally, a dozen more hijras were instructed to wait outside the door, ready to join in once they began teasing the trainer. Detailed instructions were provided to the hijras wearing hijab on how to respond when the trainer arrived and joined them. The coffee shop and its surroundings were bustling with activity during rush hour, attracting many of the invited freshers.

The trainer was dressed to the nine, donning finely pressed white trousers and his beloved yellow shirt. With perfume and roses in hand, clean-shaven and without a mustache, he confidently met the women in hijabs at the coffee shop, fulfilling his promise. Identifying the only table occupied by ladies in hijabs, the trainer effortlessly located them and took a seat in front of the group. As he pointed toward the perfumes and extended the bouquet of roses to one of the ladies, he plucked a rose from his lapel and offered it to another, affectionately stating, "Darling, I am fully aware of the charismatic charm that can make anyone fall in love with me. Please, my love, tell me, how do I appear now, clean-shaven and without a mustache? I hope I am even more handsome than when you previously saw me with a mustache."

One hijra responded, "You look like the most handsome man I have ever seen, I will snatch you from my sister."

The trainer, feeling afraid and bewildered, asked, "Excuse me?"

The trainer began to doubt the authenticity of the lady's voice. Despite her attempt to sound feminine, it was a heavy blend of female and hijra tones. She clarified that they had lost their voices after consuming spicy and contaminated food at a wedding the previous night, where they had to sing loudly. She advised him not to judge solely by their voices.

The trainer attempted to address the other lady, assuming she was Saira Banu, and asked, "Darling, can you say something? Do I look handsome to you?"

The second hijra hesitated and displayed a response from within the hijab, indicating shyness.

Undeterred, the trainer continued with hot-off-the-fire confidence, "I understand your shyness and that you may not speak here. That's why I have purchased a ticket for a Bollywood show tomorrow afternoon."

The first hijra inched closer to the trainer.

The trainer tried to distance himself from the first person, attempting to avoid causing a scene.

He inched toward the second lady and continued with the same confidence, "Darling, I know you girls prefer phone conversation rather than talking out loud face-to-face. I like that."

The second lady made efforts to resist the trainer's advances as he persisted in getting closer to her. Simultaneously, the first lady attempted to draw nearer to the trainer, but he rejected her advances. Eventually, the second lady stood up, trying to distance herself from him. The trainer and the first lady also leaped up alongside her. The commotion grew louder, and most of the public's attention hovered over the conversation and interaction between the trainer and the ladies. The second lady tried to break free from the trainer's hold, while he tried to free himself from the grasp of the first lady.

The trainer kept repeating his words and tried to get closer to the second lady, just as the first lady repeated her words and tried to draw nearer to him. Unable to continue, the trainer slapped the first lady heavily across the face, and in response, the second lady slapped the trainer. Both hijras came out of their hijabs and began abusing the trainer. At the same time, the rest of the hijras joined them in abusing and insulting the trainer.

They chased the trainer out of the coffee shop and onto the street until the trainer offered them a sizable amount of money to leave him alone and let him retrieve his parked car. The trainer noticed that his trainees were actually enjoying his humiliation, and none of them came forward to help him. In fact, some of the trainees were twisting their mustaches out of haughtiness to tease the trainer as he was being chased by the hijras. The trainer began to suspect that Tejas and JK may have conspired that situation, especially when he saw Tejas directing the rest of the hijras toward him. It was a tremendous blow to the trainer's dignity, and he felt deeply embarrassed by the incident.

The trainer, fueled by his desire for revenge and still seething from the insult inflicted upon him by the hijras, made a firm decision to take action against the trainees, particularly targeting Tejas and JK. Determined to teach them a lesson, he procured the list of trainees who were present at the coffee shop that day and devised a plan for their punishment. He issued strict orders for the trainees, emphasizing that they had violated the rules by leaving the campus without proper permission during training hours.

In response, the trainees were subjected to backbreaking field exercises, designed to push them to their limits under the scorching sun and sweltering heat. The punishments were intentionally severe, serving as a reminder of the trainer's authority and the consequences of their actions. The trainer spared no effort in making sure that the trainees experienced the consequences of their behavior.

However, the trainer's primary focus remained on finding Tejas and JK, as he was determined to deliver additional punishments directly to them. He scoured the training grounds, keeping a vigilant eye out for the two individuals who had become the primary targets of his wrath. The trainer's pursuit of justice intensified, and he eagerly awaited the opportunity to confront Tejas and JK and administer the retribution he believed they deserved.

Albeit, both Tejas and JK managed to evade the impending punishments by resorting to clever tactics. Tejas cleverly held an onion under his shoulder to artificially raise his body temperature, simulating a high fever and sickness. Meanwhile, JK resorted to ingesting Tiglium (*Jamalgota*), a potent laxative, to induce diarrhea and create the illusion of being unwell. They believed their cunning plan would grant them immunity from punishment.

But their carefully crafted scheme was short-lived, as the trainer's keen observation skills and intuition led him to ferret out the truth. The trainer found the onion and *Jamalgota* remnants in the trash outside Tejas and JK's room, exposing their deceitful ploy. With their ruse exposed, the trainer decided to shift his focus solely on punishing Tejas and JK, intending to make the consequences even more severe for their attempted deception.

Yet, an unexpected turn of events interrupted the trainer's plans. A surprise visit by the defense minister to the training school disrupted the scheduled punishments. The presence of such a distinguished figure in their midst forced the trainer to temporarily set aside his disciplinary measures.

During the defense minister's visit, Tejas and JK demonstrated remarkable bravery and courage, impressing not only the defense minister but also the trainer himself. Their exceptional display of valor surpassed that of their fellow freshers and even some of the senior trainees, earning them admiration and accolades from both the defense minister and the trainer. Recognizing their extraordinary potential, the defense minister announced an instant promotion for the trainer and praised his skill in effectively training these exceptional individuals.

Considering this newfound recognition and acclaim, the trainer abandoned his plans for further punishment and instead, Tejas and JK became his most favored trainees. The trainer rewarded them with new and challenging assignments, recognizing their unique talents and ability to overcome adversity. The tables had turned, and what was initially intended as punishment had transformed into an opportunity for growth for Tejas and JK under the trainer's guidance.

The first level of training came to an end, marking an important milestone in their journey. It was time for the trainees to disperse and embark on the next phase of their training. Some trainees would continue their training at the same base. Whereas, others would be dispatched to various regions of the country for field training, broadening their horizons and testing their skills in diverse environments.

Acknowledging his outstanding skills and leadership, the trainer received a promotion and was assigned to lead field training in the scenic town of Gulmarg in J&K. This new role brought with it greater authority and decision-making power. The trainer was given the privilege of handpicking a select group of a dozen trainees to accompany him on this challenging assignment.

Having formed a strong bond during their time together, the trainer, Tejas, and JK had developed a close friendship. Appreciating their abilities and commitment, the trainer selected them for the group, recognizing them as some of the best trainees due to their exceptional performance. The trainer's decision was a testament to the trust and camaraderie that had developed between them.

Anticipation and excitement surged through the chosen group as they readied for advanced training, eager to tackle fresh challenges and expand their capabilities under the trainer's guidance. The trainer's trust in Tejas, JK, and their peers set the stage for an adventure-filled and life-changing journey in Gulmarg.

After a brief break, the trainees were scheduled to commence their field training in the picturesque town of Gulmarg. Among them, Tejas sally forth on a unique journey as he arrived in Srinagar accompanied by his newlywed wife, Sanam. Tejas, with the hope of finding teaching training opportunities for Sanam, arranged for her temporary residence in the city. He aspired for her to secure a teaching position in one of the schools there.

Tejas eagerly resumed his field training in Gulmarg, immersing himself in the rigorous exercises and learning experiences. However, during weekends or on special holidays, he made a point to travel back to Srinagar to spend precious time with his beloved wife, Sanam. Their relationship remained a well-kept secret, known only to the trainer and JK, who had been entrusted with this private knowledge.

13. Laila's Encounter: Tejas & JK

After months of intensive training in the picturesque surroundings of Gulmarg, the trainees were assigned crucial duties alongside the serving armies, marking their transition into the field. Nevertheless, the area of their deployment presented a formidable obstacle in the shape of a surge in militant and cross-border terrorist operations.

Terrorist organizations exploited the training grounds of PoK to train individuals who would later infiltrate the Indian side of Kashmir. Disturbingly, many of these individuals were local boys from the Indian side of Kashmir, either enticed or coerced into engaging in terrorist activities within the valley. The influence of local religious figures played a role as well, as they provided shelter to these terrorists and misguided the youth in the name of jihad.

Though most ordinary citizens in the streets of Srinagar rejected violence, a small number, backed by Pakistan, enlisted vulnerable youths into militant training camps. Their objective was to sow discord and unrest in the beautiful Kashmir valley.

The individuals who incited the youth toward this self-proclaimed jihad conveniently safeguarded their own children, distancing them from the perils they encouraged others to follow. Tragically, those who fell victim to the terrorist activities in the Kashmir valley came from the most underprivileged and marginalized sections of society. This stark contrast underlined the urgent need to educate the youth, ensuring they were not misled by individuals driven by personal agendas that aimed to undermine the unity of the country.

To tackle this issue, the Ministry of Home Affairs worked alongside the Ministry of Defense and the Ministry of Education. The objective was to create a comprehensive program covering education, awareness, and welfare efforts. The program was carried out by the army personnel in the valley, who played a vital role in both border security and the well-being of J&K residents.

As part of their routine duties, the deployed army personnel took on the responsibility of educating the youth. Alongside their primary tasks of upholding national unity and security, including conducting anti-terror operations and counter-insurgency measures, they actively engaged with the local communities. They spread awareness about the repercussions of misguided ideologies and the importance of preserving peace and harmony.

The objective was to empower youth with knowledge and equip them to discern truth from falsehood, enabling them to contribute positively to society by investing in education, awareness, and welfare. This effort aimed to break the cycle of violence and create a conducive environment for growth and development in the Kashmir valley.

The dedication of deployed army personnel made the multifaceted approach effective, promoting hope and enlightenment among the youth. As they carried out their duties, they realized the weightiness of protecting the nation's borders and nurturing the next generation's minds, shaping a brighter future for J&K.

During that period, Maulana Omar held a position of great influence as the supreme leader of the Taliban in Afghanistan. The Taliban, in collaboration with Pakistan, had established a pact with the aim of liberating Kashmir from Indian control. According to this agreement, the Taliban would extend their support to Pakistan by providing militants and terrorists, while Pakistan, in turn, would facilitate the ascension of Omar's brother, Ahmed Omari, as the Caliph of a free Kashmir.

With the tightening grip of Western countries on militant activities in Afghanistan, many militants sought refuge in PoK, which served as a safe haven for their operations. Omar and his followers were highly active in the Kashmir valley, advancing their agenda in line with the objectives set forth in the pact.

This collaboration between the Taliban, Pakistan, and certain militant groups aimed to destabilize the region and pursue their goal of an independent Kashmir. The presence and activities of Omar and his associates added a front-page dimension to the ongoing tensions in the valley, further complicating the efforts to restore peace and security.

In the course of their routine patrolling and engagement with the local community, the army personnel had to visit houses in the villages of J&K. One evening, Tejas and JK's team received some suspicious information about a Muslim youth, prompting them to pay a visit to his house.

Under the cover of darkness, they arrived and Tejas took a position to provide cover while JK proceeded to knock on the front door. The door swung open, revealing an adult girl dressed entirely in black. The darkness obscured their view of each other's faces. JK, aiming his machine gun cautiously, crouched down and illuminated the area with his lantern-style flashlight. To his astonishment, he found himself captivated by the girl's cute, attractive, and beautiful face. Tejas, too, was drawn to her beauty and could not help but be intrigued.

In that instance, a voice resonated from the inner room, belonging to the girl's mother. "Laila, my daughter, who is there?" she inquired.

"Amma, please come. Two officers are here," Laila softly replied, covering her face and leaving the place to retreat to her room.

Laila's mother stepped forward, and the officers followed her inside, taking a seat. She expressed her hospitality, saying, "Sahib, please come and sit. What brings you here? We hope all is well."

JK engaged in a conversation with Laila's mother in the local Kashmiri language, conveying crucial intelligence regarding her son's involvement. Within moments, the tranquility of the evening was disrupted as two militant individuals arrived at her doorstep, seeking the whereabouts of the youth. Sensing the impending danger, Tejas and JK swiftly concealed themselves, positioning themselves strategically to provide assistance while ensuring her safety.

As the menacing voices grew louder and the threats escalated, Tejas and JK coordinated their actions with precision. They synchronized their movements, relying on their extensive training and instinctual responses. They acted swiftly and decisively, shooting and disabling the intruders to neutralize the immediate threat. Exhibiting remarkable skill and resourcefulness, Tejas and JK apprehended the militants, ensuring the safety of Laila and her mother.

Overwhelmed with gratitude, Laila and her mother expressed their heartfelt appreciation for the courage displayed by the two soldiers.

Laila, captivated by JK's remarkable bravery, was not only drawn to his chiseled physique but also deeply touched by his compassion and concern for her mother's well-being. She recognized the immense sacrifice and selflessness of these soldiers in protecting her family, leaving a lasting impression on her.

Laila's enchanting beauty, exuding an aura of elegance and allure, was undeniable. While JK could not help but feel a magnetic attraction toward her, Tejas, understanding his comrade's sentiment, skillfully used his words to highlight Laila's admirable qualities, aiming to uplift the spirits of his fellow soldier amidst their demanding duties.

One sunny day, during their routine patrol along a rugged hilly slope, Tejas mischievously seized an opportunity to tease JK about Laila. Pointing at a piece of paper, he playfully taunted, "Hey, baradar! Look, she sent you a letter."

In a playful strive, JK started chasing Tejas, determined to seize the paper and put an end to the sarcasm. With a mix of determination and humor, he pleaded, "Yes, baradar!! This is not fair. Please show it or stop teasing me."

This lively exchange continued a couple of times, as JK valiantly attempted to catch up to Tejas. However, his efforts proved futile, as the elusive Tejas managed to stay just out of his reach. Undeterred, JK persevered, determined to seize the paper and uncover its contents.

On their third encounter, a twist of fate intervened. JK, powered by a surge of determination, finally succeeded in snatching the paper from Tejas. However, in a moment of unfortunate misfortune, JK lost his footing on the treacherous hilly slope. Helplessly, he began a rapid descent down the opposite side of the hill, his heart pounding with adrenaline.

In a tumultuous cascade of events, JK's descent came to an abrupt halt as he collided with an apple tree. The impact left him unconscious, his body coming to rest amidst a picturesque apple orchard, surrounded by the sweet scent of ripe fruit.

Laila was engaged in play with a group of children as she diligently guarded her apple orchard when a resounding noise of something falling into the orchard startled them. With urgency, Laila and the children hastened toward the source of the sound, discovering a fallen individual, like an apple from the tree. Promptly, they approached to offer their assistance, only to witness copious amounts of blood emanating from a gash on the person's arm. Laila promptly aided the injured party in assuming a proper supine position, and to her astonishment, she recognized the wounded individual as JK.

Moved by a sense of urgency, Laila swiftly removed her headscarf and issued a commanding directive to the children, urging them to fetch a hakim from a nearby location. In the midst of her actions, JK regained consciousness. Overwhelmed with joy upon seeing Laila before him, he discreetly feigned sleep while silently observing her every movement.

In a fleeting moment, JK became captivated by the vision of Laila's unbound tresses cascading freely in the air, momentarily transporting him to a realm akin to paradise. As she gently held his arm, delicately wrapping the scarf around his injured limb, her touch breathed life into him, and he surreptitiously admired her innate innocence and beauty.

In due course, the hakim arrived, administering proper treatment to JK's wound and prescribing necessary medication. Before departing, the hakim reassured JK, stating, "Son, fret not. I have applied potent medicine to your wound, and you shall recover swiftly."

JK extended his heartfelt gratitude and appreciation to Laila. In response, Laila gestured to him, urging him not to mention it, and tenderly placed a hand over his mouth. She considered it her duty to provide aid. Witnessing this heartfelt exchange, the children present modestly closed their eyes, pretending not to have witnessed the tender scene before them.

Meanwhile, Tejas, who had been trailing behind JK, witnessed the entire episode unfold before him. Seeing Laila's care for JK, he chose to withdraw secretly into the shadows, content in knowing that his loyal comrade was in good hands. When the commotion settled and JK and Laila shared a brief yet meaningful exchange, Tejas decided to playfully mimic the dramatic fall from the slope.

Reacting swiftly, everyone rushed to Tejas's aid, and JK, the loyal friend, was there to assist him. Tejas could not resist teasing Laila, playfully urging her to don a headscarf and then remove it to wrap around his wounded arm. Amidst laughter and banter, they all understood Tejas's mischievous intent. Laila, her cheeks flushing with a delightful shyness, gracefully excused herself from the scene, leaving a lasting impression on both soldiers.

As JK playfully chased Tejas, their eyes caught a final glimpse of Laila's retreating figure, her shy demeanor lingering in their thoughts. Eventually, they returned to the camp, carrying with them the memory of an unexpected encounter that had touched their hearts in ways they could not fully comprehend.

In the confines of the army camp, Tejas could not contain his admiration for Laila, and his fellow colleagues could not help but notice the special sparkle in his eyes whenever her name was mentioned. Whispers of love and affection spread through the camp, leading to assumptions that Tejas had fallen head over heels for Laila.

One pleasant evening, as they gathered under the starlit sky, enjoying the camaraderie and indulging in drinks and merriment, Tejas seized the moment to express his sentiments. He began to sing the popular melody, "*Andheri Raat Mein….,*" his voice resonating through the night air. Initially, his comrades assumed he was serenading Laila, pouring his heart out through the lyrics.

However, midway through the song, Tejas playfully beckoned JK to join him in the performance. With a mischievous glint in his eyes, Tejas encouraged JK to sing, knowing full well the admiration he had for Laila. The lyrics now swelled with praises and adoration for her, the melody carrying the unspoken emotions that had taken root within JK's heart.

In that moment, the truth was unveiled, and the gathering came to realize the depth of JK's feelings for Laila. A mixture of surprise and understanding swept through their comrades, as they embraced the realization that love had woven its intricate threads amidst the challenges and camaraderie of their shared journey.

Love bloomed in JK's heart like an unexpected wildflower on the battlefield, a delicate contrast to the rugged terrain of war.

ANDHERI RAAT MEIN
(*Voice*: Mr. Rakesh Singh)

Andheri raat mein tumne kya dekha hai
-kya dekha hai, kya dekha hai, anh?
pura chand ko tumne kya dekha hai
-pura chand ko, wo kaisa dikhega anh?
ashma mein kyon dekhe pyare humne use jami pe dekha hai
-are bangru ye lagta hai pagla gaya hai ise kuch tonic shonic pilao
-guru ye sab tonic nahi chalegi ise to love ki photonic mil gayi hai
-o ye baat hai!! ....

Andheri raat mein tumne kya dekha hai
pura chand ko tumne kya dekha hai
andheri raat mein tumne kya dekha hai
pura chand ko tumne kya dekha hai
ashma mein kyon dekhe pyare humne use jami pe dekha hai

Jab zulf wo lehraye
jab zulf wo lehraye, wahin chha jati ghatayen

Jab payal wo khankaye, sare ho jate deewane
sare ho jate deewane

Andheri raat mein tumne kya dekha hai
pura chand ko tumne kya dekha hai

Jab balkha ke wo jaye
jab balkha ke wo jaye, kitno ki maut ho jaye

Jab muska ke wo aaye, mehfil me jaan aa jaye
mehfil me jaan aa jaye

Andheri raat mein tumne kya dekha hai
pura chand ko tumne kya dekha hai....

Sometimes, during their routine patrols through the villages and surrounding areas, Tejas and JK would find themselves passing by Laila's house. Whenever Laila's observant mother caught sight of the soldiers, she would graciously extend an invitation for them to enter their humble abode and share a cup of tea.

These serendipitous encounters granted Tejas, JK, and Laila opportunities to engage in conversation and forge connections. With keen insight into the soft spot that JK and Laila held for each other, Tejas would often include Laila's mother in their discussions, creating an environment that allowed JK and Laila to enjoy moments of privacy. In these precious instances, their shared experiences fostered a deeper understanding and closeness between them.

As time passed, Tejas seized every chance to playfully tease JK about his clandestine and secluded meetings with Laila. With mischievous delight, he would jest and make light-hearted remarks, ensuring that JK's secret encounters were not overlooked or forgotten.

Laila was the daughter of a social worker residing in a village near the army camp. Her father had limited involvement in politics.

However, as the situation in the valley worsened, he found himself drawn into the political realm. He began residing in another part of the valley and seldom returned to his hometown. Although some believed he had abandoned his family, he held a deep affection for his children.

Displeased with the approaches taken by the major political parties in restoring peace to the valley, Laila's father made a head-turner decision. He resolved to contest in the assembly elections as an independent candidate. Her father was driven by a grand vision to broaden his political influence throughout the valley. With his eyes set on the forthcoming election, he directed his family to relocate to the place where he was politically active. He believed that having his family by his side would provide him with support and assistance.

In a sudden turn of events, the family swiftly shifted to their father's new abode, accepting the changes that awaited them in this unfamiliar environment.

14. Confronting Terror: Tejas's Demise

Securing the border area in the snowy mountains is akin to the vigilant sentinels of the frozen frontier, where every snowflake is a silent witness to their indefatigable watch.

Guarding, patrolling, and protecting the border area in the snowy mountains of J&K presented the Indian army with their most arduous and challenging task. Their soldiers consistently confronted the malicious intentions of cunning militants and snipers, along with terrorists, who aimed to exploit any chances for infiltration. Furthermore, they faced the ever-looming threat of attacks from Pakistan's border action teams. Alongside these security concerns, they battled extreme cold weather, inhospitable terrains, and treacherous deep gorges on their side of the border.

The cloudy and snowy conditions along the Line of Control (LoC) often resulted in poor visibility, making it difficult for soldiers to even see their comrades standing just a few meters away. Despite these challenges, the Indian army remained steadfast in their mission to protect against nefarious Pakistani designs. In addition to countering infiltrating terrorists and enemy forces, they also had to contend with the harsh realities of snow, cold weather, and challenging terrains during their long-range patrols along the LoC.

The intelligence agencies provided occasional alerts about the presence of infiltrating militants in the valley, prompting the Indian army to swiftly take action. This time, the intelligence received alarming information about high-level militants targeting a prominent Indian figure. Their objective was to cause maximum destruction, with a high-level Indian political leader as the likely target. The repercussions of such an attack would be catastrophic, plunging the Indian side into chaos and turmoil.

Faced with these severe threats, the Indian army displayed unflappable resolve, ready to confront any challenges endangering the peace and security of the region. Their unfaltering commitment and indomitable spirit were tested as they served as the front line, safeguarding their nation's borders. As the untimely heavy snowfall blanketed the valley, a large group of terrorists seized the opportunity to infiltrate the Indian side. Exploiting the assumption that the Indian military would be unprepared during this unexpected weather, the militants aimed to carry out a fatalistic attack. Their nefarious plan involved targeting an Indian political leader, as well as the army camp stationed near Srinagar.

The intelligence agencies swiftly relayed crucial information to the Army, underscoring the presence of a notorious figure named Omari in the Gulmarg and Srinagar region. In response, the responsibility of the search and attack mission was entrusted to the capable hands of Officer Pitambar, the newly appointed field officer who also served as the trainer.

Recognizing the seriousness of the situation, Officer Pitambar meticulously handpicked a team of highly skilled senior military personnel. In addition, he recognized the exceptional capabilities of Tejas and JK, who were the epitome of excellence among the incumbents. Their unique skills and expertise made them the perfect fit to complement the senior military personnel. With their outstanding abilities and a track record that spoke for itself, Tejas and JK were the only ones who could match the caliber of the experienced soldiers. Together, this carefully chosen team of talented individuals possessed the necessary prowess and cohesion to face the challenges ahead and accomplish the mission successfully.

As the operation loomed on the horizon, the team braced themselves for the challenges that awaited them in the treacherous snowy terrain. The harsh cold and icy conditions presented formidable challenges, but their determination to defend their nation and foil the terrorist plot amped up their resolve. With their training and camaraderie as their pillars of strength, they embarked on the mission, ready to confront the dangers that lay ahead.

The senior military personnel had wasted no time in subjecting Tejas and JK to a harsh initiation during their travel in the military vehicle to the target camp. Their intentions were clear - to belittle the newcomers for their lack of prior experience in military raids on covert grounds. Relentlessly mocking them, they aimed to instill fear in Tejas and JK by recounting tales of inexperienced operatives meeting their demise at the hands of terrorists. They even spoke of a previous operation where the boss had successfully subdued militants, but at the cost of sacrificing his own inexperienced personnel.

In their view, Pitambar, their leader, was exploiting these novices as bait to divert the militants' attention during the ongoing top-secret mission. The senior officials taunted the young recruits, sharing their inexperience in this harsh environment, likening them to newborns in need of constant care. They ominously joked that the terrorists would be the ones to feed them with bullets, and if they managed to survive, they would be rewarded with celebratory 'snow shakes.'

The journey in the military van, despite being relatively short in distance, felt like an eternity for the newly recruited personnel. The weight of anticipation and the relentless taunting had taken its toll. Upon arrival at the local camp, Pitambar emerged from another vehicle to address the soldiers. He swiftly organized them into smaller groups, instructing them to disperse and surround the target area, effectively sealing it off. Tejas, JK, and a few others were assigned to Pitambar's subgroup.

Undeterred by the harsh conditions of thick snow and high altitude, the search operation pressed on. Tejas and JK, despite their initial fears and the daunting weather, braced themselves for the challenges that awaited them in this unforgiving terrain. It was a trial by fire, where their mettle would be tested, and their determination would define their destiny.

After a while, Pitambar and his subgroup came across a gathering of individuals dressed in Muslim clerical attire. They were exiting a small mosque and setting off along a snowy footpath toward an undisclosed destination, presumably for a wedding. The group consisted of a Kaji, a bride, a groom, as well as male and female relatives, all adhering to the customs of a Muslim marriage, with the women wearing hijabs. Unbeknownst to the military, these individuals were actually males attempting to escape under the guise of civilian Muslim religious customs. They had made the erroneous assumption that their hideout in this remote and isolated region, with its unseasonal snowfall, would remain undetected. However, the military had indeed nosed out their presence, forcing them to hastily flee with only a limited number of weapons, arms, and ammunition.

The military personnel had their suspicions, prompting them to stop the group and conduct an inquiry and search operation. At first, the individuals tried to convince the military personnel that they were innocent civilians involved in a religious marriage ceremony. They argued that questioning them would violate the moral ethics of the Indian army and emphasized that Muslim law prohibits interference in their religious rituals. Despite their pleas, the military persisted with their inquiry and search.

Tejas, sensing something amiss, approached one of the individuals in an attempt to establish eye contact. The person's demeanor raised Tejas's suspicions. Just as Tejas was about to conduct a thorough search, the man forcefully pushed him away and swiftly began skating across the snow, heading toward the dense forest. In a synchronized motion, the remaining suspected individuals also started skating in different directions, attempting to evade capture. The military personnel swiftly gave chase, their pursuit unfolding amidst the snowy landscape.

As the chase ensued, it became apparent that the number of militants outnumbered the army personnel. Some militants managed to escape without being trailed by the army. Tejas, JK, Pitambar, and the other officers found themselves scattered, each independently tailing the fleeing militants in various directions. Amidst the chaos and uncertainty, their training and instincts guided their actions as they fervently pursued the militants through the unforgiving terrain.

Tejas tracked the person who had started fleeing first. Eventually, he managed to catch up to the individual, resulting in a close chase and subsequent fight. Tejas targeted the militant's lower leg with a strike, causing him to collapse and roll downhill on the slope. Seizing the opportunity, Tejas attempted to grab the militant's neck, but his hand slipped, inadvertently removing the person's face mask, clothes, and goggles. The two adversaries found themselves in close proximity.

To Tejas' astonishment, he discovered that the person he had apprehended was none other than Omari, the PoK terror boss. Initially taken aback by the encounter with the deadliest terrorist during his first military operation, Tejas, with all his might, took the bull by the horns.

A lengthy battle ensued between the two combatants. Unfortunately for the militant, he had only a limited supply of weapons and ammunition. Their hideout had not anticipated a military operation and had to be abandoned hastily. Consequently, they were unable to acquire their heavier weaponry. Omari was armed with only small-range pistols, lethal knives, and a few small handball bombs. Undeterred, Tejas fearlessly faced Omari's attacks.

The army's objective was to capture the militants alive whenever possible, with neutralization reserved as a last resort, when an army member's life was in imminent danger. Collecting valuable intelligence on the militants' activities and their influence over impressionable young residents of J&K was all-important. An integral part of the army's mission was to build goodwill and nurture trust within the local community. Rather than asserting control over the population, the army's presence in J&K was geared toward providing essential services. It included border protection, ensuring safety and security, and extending support in critical areas such as healthcare, education, and the overall well-being of the local residents. By prioritizing the people's welfare and ensuring a secure environment, the army aimed to make a positive impact and inspire confidence among the residents of J&K.

Tejas valiantly battled against Omari, absorbing his blows without resorting to extreme tactics to neutralize him. He intended to preserve Omari's life so that justice could be served through the Indian judicial system, serving as a lesson for other militants. As Omari's arsenal dwindled and frustration set in, he resorted to taunting and issuing challenges to Tejas.

Omari argued that the Indian Army's perceived bravery was merely a result of superior armament and resources. He claimed that the militant groups possessed greater courage and power, lacking only the technological and armed support that the Indian Army enjoyed; otherwise, they could free J&K in a couple of months. According to Omari's reasoning, the people of J&K were inherently supportive of an independent Azad Kashmir and were simply awaiting the opportune moment to switch allegiance.

Thus, Omari contended that the Indian military's courage stemmed primarily from their reliance on modern armed technology and abundant resources, attributing their control over the valley to these factors. Without such advantages, he maintained that the Indian forces would be outmatched by the militants on an individual level. On a personal level, Omari challenged Tejas to demonstrate his bravery without weapons, confident that he could defeat him in an instant. He further vowed to take Tejas captive across the border and subject him to enslavement.

Tejas fearlessly accepted Omari's challenge, commencing a fierce battle on the snowy mountain. As the fight progressed, Tejas soon recognized that Omari was trained in black belt karate, prompting him to stay on guard. However, the realization also filled Tejas with excitement, as he finally had the opportunity to showcase his own black belt skills within a military context. Although Tejas had been a black belt runner-up in the All India level competition, he had been unable to compete in the finals due to a knee injury sustained during a practice session. Nonetheless, he was widely expected to become the national champion.

Positioning himself as if this were his final black belt championship, Tejas engaged Omari in a high-stakes duel on the snowy hillside. In a fraction of time, Tejas emerged victorious, asserting, "Even without arms, we are superior to you fugitives. If my government allowed it, it would not take a couple of months, but merely a couple of days to not only reclaim Pakistan, but also have your entire Afghanistan at our feet. However, unfortunately, we have no intentions of conquering such hellish countries."

Omari conceded defeat, and before he could resort to any further trickery or self-harm, Tejas swiftly gained control over him and administered a neck sedative. Within moments, Omari succumbed to unconsciousness. Making preparations to transport Omari back to the camp, Tejas asserted, "Listen, my friend, I am now enslaving you and my government will keep you as a slave! Let's go."

The administration of the sedative injection proved to be a highly effective method of establishing authority over the enemy, particularly in situations involving transportation. With Omari rendered unconscious, Tejas promptly lifted him onto his back and descended the slope with grace, swiftly heading toward the camp while promptly alerting his team. Meanwhile, Pitambar and JK disembarked from their vehicle and advanced toward Tejas on foot, while he raced toward them on skates, determined and swift.

As they closed in on one another, Tejas noticed a militant concealed in a strategic position, readying to unleash a volley of bullets upon Pitambar and JK. In a split second, as Pitambar, JK, and Tejas drew near, Tejas observed a bullet hurtling toward his comrades. In a moment of selfless bravery, Tejas instinctively intervened, thrust them aside and absorbed the random onslaught of bullets onto his chest. In response, the remaining army personnel swiftly pursued and neutralized the militant. Subsequently, Tejas crumpled and fell to the ground, weakened by the wounds inflicted upon him.

A soldier taking a bullet to save his comrades is like a human shield, standing strong in the line of fire to protect the hearts beating beside him.

Pitambar and JK stood in stunned disbelief, their minds reeling from Tejas's remarkable act of saving them while carrying another individual on his back, potentially an injured soldier. Their immediate instinct was to rush to Tejas's aid, but as he fell to the ground, losing consciousness, they realized the gravity of the situation. United in their resolve, they provided support to both Tejas and the unidentified individual he had valiantly carried. The duo were unaware of his identity.

As they examined him more closely, a deep shock reverberated through Pitambar and JK. They came face to face with an unimaginable truth—it was none other than India's foremost enemy, Omari himself. Pitambar's heart swelled with immense pride, for Tejas's remarkable achievement had been accomplished under his command. However, this pride was accompanied by a sense of guilt, as they understood that Tejas had taken a bullet upon himself to safeguard their lives, now teetering on the precipice between life and death.

As moments passed, Tejas gradually regained consciousness, yet his breath grew increasingly faint. Faced with the presence of Pitambar, JK, and Omari, Tejas summoned his remaining strength. With a determined gaze, he reached for the bravery medal bestowed by his grandma, extending it toward JK. His hand trembled as he clasped

JK's, conveying a reflective message of trust and responsibility. Tejas leaned in, lightly brushing Omari's forehead, signifying closure and resolution. In his parting act, he handed the medal to JK, saying, "Hey baradar!, please bring him to justice. *Jai Hind.*" It was a moment of intense emotion and undying commitment.

A soldier on the verge of death is like a fading star, its brilliant light dimming, but its legacy still shining in the night sky.

With that, Tejas released his last breath, his noble spirit transcending as he left behind a legacy of unflagging patriotism and selfless sacrifice. The same boy who was found in a bin, now had to his credit a death of valor, making him immortal.

Overwhelmed by guilt and sadness, Pitambar and JK tussled with the loss of Tejas. The weight of their emotions was heavy, knowing that the irreplaceable damage had been done. Yet, amidst the sorrow, they could not help but recognize Tejas's unparalleled courage. Single-handedly, he had captured the country's most formidable enemy, displaying unmatched bravery. Tejas had made the ultimate sacrifice, giving his own life to protect his boss and colleague, leaving behind a legacy of selflessness that would forever be etched in their hearts.

With the imminent threat of militant attacks and an attempted rescue of Omari, the military personnel meticulously prepared for his transport to the nearest base camp prison. Meanwhile, Tejas's lifeless body was tenderly placed in a separate vehicle, a solemn tribute to his ultimate sacrifice. Intense debates ensued between Pitambar and JK, centered on Tejas's undying bravery. JK passionately argued that the only path to avenge their friend's death was to immediately eliminate Omari during the journey to the base camp. Pitambar, however, held steadfast to military ethics, torn between sentimentality for Tejas, who had saved his life, and his duty-bound obligations.

JK further contended that allowing Omari to reach the base camp would provide him opportunities to evade justice, potentially enabling his men to plan a jailbreak or allowing him to continue militant activities from behind bars. Thus, JK believed that neutralizing Omari before reaching the base camp was imperative. Pitambar, forbidding JK from taking the law into his own hands, emphasized the need to trust in the Indian judiciary and legal system.

During the heated exchange, Pitambar reminded JK of Tejas's final wish to bring Omari to justice through proper legal channels. In a defiant response, JK asserted that killing Omari on the spot would fulfill their friend's last desire for justice. The tension escalated, and it seemed as though JK, consumed by his emotions, was on the verge of taking Omari's life, who lay unconscious before them. Sensing the perilous situation, Pitambar swiftly administered a sedative to JK's neck, rendering him unconscious. Commanding the personnel to transfer the unconscious JK to another vehicle, Pitambar ensured his safe journey to the base camp.

As the military convoy reached the base camp, news of Omari's capture, the notorious terrorist leader and brother of the Taliban ruler, Omar, quickly made headlines. The revelation struck a chord of embarrassment for both Pakistan and the Taliban, a moment of undeniable disgrace. Amid this tumultuous acknowledgment, Pitambar was overwhelmed with praise and accolades for his remarkable bravery and achievement. Yet, beneath the surface of these accolades, a subtle unease lingered within him, like a whispered reminder of his misplaced honor.

In the midst of the media's adulation, Pitambar couldn't help but feel a faint pang in his neck, an instinctive reaction to the hollow praises that rained upon him. Time and again, his thoughts were transported back to the haunting flashbacks of Tejas's valiant actions, how he fearlessly brought Omari to Pitambar and selflessly saved his life, at the ultimate cost of sacrificing his own. However, consumed by the allure of his fame, Pitambar overlooked the depth of Tejas's bravery and sacrifice.

During interviews and public addresses, Pitambar spoke at length about the meticulous military preparations, the strategic planning, and the successful mission to eliminate the militants. He briefly mentioned Tejas, portraying him as one of the brave soldiers who lost their lives during the encounter. Yet, it seemed as though the true magnitude of Tejas's selflessness was overshadowed, as all the credit and glory seemed to gravitate toward Pitambar, the leader of the military operation.

JK, upon seeing Pitambar exploiting his dearest friend's sacrifice on television, confronted him about his cowardice in exploiting Tejas' selflessness. He called Pitambar, determined to challenge him for his deceitful actions and threatened to expose him to higher authorities for his false claims. Furthermore, JK dared Pitambar to protect Omari, stating, "I will eliminate Omari even if you or any Indian government official attempts to shield him."

Attempting to dismiss the threats, Pitambar chose to ignore JK's words. However, JK persisted, proclaiming, "I will defy all laws and orders, and I will break every jail if necessary to locate and exact vengeance upon Omari for the death of my closest friend, who sacrificed his own life to save me."

Pitambar, daringly reminding JK of his obligations as a military professional, asserted his authority, saying, "Do not forget that you are bound by military ethics. I am your superior. Attend to your duties."

In response, JK matched the intensity of Pitambar's tone, declaring, "I am well aware of ethics. Even if Omari manages to escape to Pakistan or find refuge with the Taliban, I will relentlessly pursue him and ensure his demise. This has become my sole mission."

JK challenged Pitambar, vowing to expose his wrongdoing and expressing his determination to eliminate Omari, regardless of the cost. JK promptly reported the true sequence of events to the higher-ranking officials. He recounted how Tejas had fearlessly and alone captured Omari at the snowy hilltop, subsequently bringing him down to their location. JK revealed the tragic truth of how Tejas had made the ultimate sacrifice, losing his own life while protecting both JK and Pitambar from the militant assault.

As a result, a thorough investigation was launched at a high-level, uncovering inconsistencies and confusion within Pitambar's claims. Ultimately, eyewitness testimony confirmed the accuracy of JK's account—Tejas had indeed single-handedly apprehended Omari and tragically lost his life while ensuring the safety of JK and Pitambar. The truth revealed Tejas's genuine heroism and sacrifice, exposing inaccuracies in Pitambar's earlier assertions.

As the successful military operation had been effectively led by Pitambar, he was pardoned in the inquiry. However, he received a stern warning, emphasizing that he should refrain from discrediting the true claimant for personal gain in the future. The official account of the fight and the capture of the terrorist boss by Tejas, along with his ultimate sacrifice to save his colleagues and superiors, was broadcast nationwide. Tejas' remarkable bravery and courage were lauded at the national level, instantly turning him into a hero for millions.

At the army headquarters in Srinagar, Tejas was accorded a state salute, where his wife, Sanam, was given the opportunity to visit him one final time. Subsequently, Tejas' body was transported to India Gate in Delhi to receive national honors. A military helicopter came to the village, inviting surviving family or guardians to join a national tribute in Delhi, honoring Tejas' sacrifice.

Amidst the smoldering embers of communal riots, the villagers returned from the cremation ground, their hearts heavy with grief from bidding farewell to Masterji. A grievous shock swept through their community upon receiving news that an army helicopter had arrived to transport grandma, bearing the solemn invitation to attend the national honor ceremony for Tejas, who had fallen as a martyr in service to the nation. The dual loss of Masterji and Tejas, occurring almost simultaneously, plunged the community into a state of disbelief at the cruel hand of fate that had snatched away two beloved souls simultaneously.

Grandma was already engulfed in sorrow following the loss of Masterji. The news of Tejas' demise came as a devastating blow, leaving her shell-shocked. Within a matter of days, she had endured two heartbreaking losses, with no surviving family members to lean on in her old age. The simultaneous occurrence of these tragic events was unfathomable to her. However, amidst the anguish, she found solace in her pride for her martyr children.

Grandma was gracefully escorted into the awaiting army helicopter, which whisked her away to India Gate in Delhi. Accompanied by compassionate army officers, she was granted the opportunity to bid a final farewell to Tejas, beholding his lifeless body one last time. The solemn occasion was marked by the resounding echoes of a 21-gun salute, paying tribute to the fallen martyr, Tejas.

Following this poignant ceremony, grandma was entrusted with a microphone, symbolizing her chance to address the assembled press, who had gathered to witness the solemn event. Overwhelmed with emotion, her voice quivering with tears. However, she gathered the strength to speak, uttering heartfelt words, "I have devoted my children to the cause of communal service and national duty."

In a moment of vulnerability, as the microphone slipped from her trembling grasp, a compassionate woman constable provided support, ensuring grandma's continued presence. Summoning great courage, grandma proclaimed, "I am filled with immense pride for all my children, who served our nation with honesty and, in their commitment, did not hesitate to offer the ultimate sacrifice."

With eyes uplifted toward the heavens, she expressed her heartfelt lamentation to God, "Dear God, I wish I had been blessed with more children to selflessly offer in service to our beloved motherland." In a final gesture of patriotism, grandma proudly saluted the national flag, her voice resounding as she fervently cried out, "*Jai Hind !*"

The echoes of Tejas's heroic actions reverberated throughout the nation, leaving an indelible mark on the collective consciousness. In a resounding tribute to his valor and selflessness, the Indian government made a momentous announcement. The military academy, situated at the district headquarters, a hallowed institution responsible for nurturing the future defenders of the nation, would be renamed in honor of Tejas. This symbolic gesture served as a testament to his extraordinary courage, immortalizing his name and ensuring that his legacy would endure for generations to come.

Not content with mere words, the government further planned to erect a majestic statue of Tejas within the revered grounds of the academy. This physical embodiment of his unwavering resolve and exemplary bravery would stand tall, serving as a perpetual reminder of his profound impact and inspiring generations of aspiring warriors to embody his virtuous spirit. It was a gesture of gratitude and reverence, acknowledging Tejas as a beacon of inspiration and a guiding light for future cadets who would walk the hallowed halls of the institution.

Therefore, Tejas's legacy would forever remain etched in the annals of the nation's history, an everlasting symbol of courage, sacrifice, and commitment to serving the motherland.

15. Laila's Abduction: Omari's Liberation

Sometimes, JK contemplated launching an attack on Omari while he was imprisoned, but his attempts proved unsuccessful. Whenever JK confronted Pitambar, the burden of his guilt for defending Omari and using Tejas's sacrifice to his advantage made him avoid facing JK. Eventually, Pitambar devised a cunning plan to have JK transferred to a remote and arduous military camp, perhaps to distance himself from the guilt and confrontations.

As time passed, JK's restlessness grew with each passing day as the Indian government postponed Omari's execution. Thus far, the government lacked substantial direct evidence to take decisive action against Omari. Additionally, Omari made efforts to assert his Indian citizenship, but the Indian government contested his claim. Despite being an illegal immigrant, the court mandated that the Indian government gather concrete evidence to support the case against Omari. Consequently, the trial faced delays, and he remained confined in an Indian base camp jail pending further hearings.

Following Tejas' demise, JK paid a visit to Sanam's residence in Srinagar. He committed to seeking justice for his friend's sacrifice, vowing to punish Omari regardless of the consequences. Sharing anecdotes of Tejas's unparalleled bravery, JK recounted how he fearlessly confronted the terrorist boss alone, apprehended him, and brought him down from the treacherous hilltop to safety. Tragically, JK experienced the irreparable loss of his friend, who had selflessly saved him and made the ultimate sacrifice in service to their beloved motherland. JK pledged his own life to Tejas' memory, affirming that he would one day bring justice to his sacrifice by eliminating Omari and other terrorists.

With numerous friends and relatives in Srinagar, JK utilized his connections to assist Sanam after she completed her teacher training. Through his efforts, he secured a permanent teaching position for her at a middle school in Srinagar. While he was stationed near Srinagar, he made occasional visits to support her whenever possible. However, due to subsequent transfers to different locations, it became increasingly challenging for him to visit her. Nonetheless, JK relied on updates from his friends and relatives to stay informed about Sanam's well-being. Occasionally, he would reach out to her through a neighbor's phone to ensure he knew her whereabouts and offer his support.

In the recently concluded election, none of the major political parties managed to secure a majority to form a government in the state of J&K. As a result, political instability gripped the valley, exacerbating the existing turmoil. Remarkably, Laila's father emerged victorious in the state assembly election as an independent candidate.

The right-wing party found itself lacking one candidate to secure a majority. In an attempt to bridge this gap, they initially sought to entice Laila's father with bribes, hoping to persuade him to join their party. However, to block the opposition party from forming a government, the right-wing party decided to back him as their chief ministerial candidate, even if he chose not to formally join their party. Consequently, Laila's father assumed the esteemed position of chief minister of J&K. Upon assuming the role, the family members were summoned to shift to the chief ministerial residence for security reasons.

Meanwhile, the militants keenly observed the political developments in the valley. Recognizing a chance, they hatched a sinister plot to kidnap Laila, the daughter of the newly appointed and inexperienced chief minister. Their plan was to strike when her family was on the way to the chief ministerial residence. Succumbing to their scheme, Laila was tragically kidnapped and forcibly taken to PoK.

Despite his efforts, JK was unable to reach Omari, who was confined within a heavily fortified military base camp prison. JK's transfer to a new location made it impossible for him to return to his previous camp and continue pursuing Omari. This inability to avenge Tejas's untimely death weighed heavily on JK, leaving him deeply disturbed. To exacerbate his distress, JK's restlessness intensified upon learning about the terrorists' kidnapping of Laila.

JK was suspicious that Laila's kidnapping was somehow connected to Omari. His cynicism was confirmed when the militants thrust the condition upon the Indian government, demanding the exchange of Laila for Omari. JK vehemently protested to the higher authorities, urging them not to release Omari in exchange for Laila.

Despite his fervent prayers for Laila's safety, JK's conscience prevented him from accepting the demand to set Omari free. He made efforts to persuade the officials by proposing an alternative solution. JK argued that if the Indian government granted him permission for a covert mission to cross the border, he could locate and safely rescue Laila. He vehemently protested and appealed to the officials not to release a dangerous terrorist like Omari. He stressed that such an action would set a perilous precedent by exchanging kidnapped children of Indian VIPs for the release of militants.

The officials scornfully rejected JK's proposals for rescuing and bringing Laila back from Pakistan, subjecting him to ridicule and bullying for what they perceived as foolishness. This incident left JK deeply unsettled, rendering him unable to focus on his work. Engulfed in an internal struggle, he found himself at a crossroads, grappling with a momentous decision. Recollections of Tejas's courageous act of apprehending Omari and his ultimate sacrifice for the nation weighed heavily on JK's mind, now seeming futile in light of Omari's impending release.

The right-wing party, which held power in the central government, played a key role in the occurring events. Moreover, Laila's maternal uncle held the esteemed position of Union State Home Minister. In a closed-door meeting with the Prime Minister, he issued a stern warning, cautioning that failure to release Omari in exchange for Laila's freedom could jeopardize the survival of both the central and J&K governments. Eventually, succumbing to the pressure, the central government conceded and agreed to the deal.

JK became disillusioned with politicians who appeared to exploit military sacrifices for their vested interests, perceiving that dedication and hard work within the military held no value in their eyes. The politicization of military sacrifice for political gains left JK in a state of dilemma. He questioned whether he should continue his service in the army, as it appeared to impede his ability to serve the nation impartially and effectively.

Adding to his distress, many military personnel began mocking him for his suggestion to rescue and safely bring Laila back from Pakistan. Ultimately, JK made the difficult decision to take a break from his military duties. He left the military camp for a period, seeking solitude to reflect on his choices and gain clarity amid the disheartening circumstances.

In accordance with the agreed-upon deal, the militants brought Laila to the India-Pakistan border, while Indian government personnel accompanied Omari to the same location. The border was chosen as the designated exchange point by the militants. During the exchange, Omari was handcuffed with his hands in front, while Laila's hands were bound behind her back. The exchange commenced with Laila walking from the militants' side, while Omari walked from the Indian side.

As Omari caught sight of the gorgeous, cute, and beautiful Laila approaching during the exchange, a sinister notion crept into his mind. His sanity slipped away, and he began to employ cunning tactics while they walked toward each other. Drawn by her captivating beauty, he found himself irresistibly attracted to her. Upon reaching the midpoint, he abruptly turned and used his handcuffed hand to secure her head, ensnaring her within his grip. Walking backward toward the militants, he exploited her presence as a means to deter any potential attack from the Indian personnel. With Laila unintentionally becoming his accomplice, he managed to evade the Indian forces and escape with her across the border to PoK.

In those unsettling moments when he held her head with his handcuffed hand, Omari felt an unusual allure, sensing the warmth of her breath near his heart. However, Laila, still reeling from the shock of the situation, was discomfited by his proximity. Moments earlier, she had expected her impending freedom and a reunion with her family, but her fate had drastically shifted, dragging her deeper into the abyss.

Omari had two types of plans for Laila. Firstly, as he was smitten by her beauty, his primary desire was to marry her and keep her as his mistress. Secondly, if she refused his proposal, he intended to use her as bait to negotiate for the release of a group of terrorists held by the Indian government. However, Laila did not appreciate his attitude and declined his marriage proposal.

In response to her refusal, he resorted to using force to compel her to agree with his wishes. Despite all his attempts, she refused to comply, stating that she would rather choose to die. During this process, witnessing her immovable self-esteem, he began to develop respect for her and softened his approach. He gradually realized that he was in love with her and made a promise to win her heart before marrying her. He even went as far as declaring his love for her to his organization.

Upon declaring his love for Laila, Omari decided to respect her pride and position as his future bride. He believed that everyone in PoK, including himself, should treat her as a princess and the future Queen of the liberated Kashmir valley from India. Therefore, he ordered that Laila should be kept near his room in the Royal Palace and be accorded royal honors.

However, Omari faced a dilemma influenced by radical Muslim thinking. According to such beliefs, women are often expected to wear a strict full-body covering known as the hijab to minimize their exposure to the outside world. Omari pondered the issue of how to distinguish Laila from the rest of the women in the palace if she were to adopt this form of dress.

Omari's trusted aide suggested an alternative approach to handling Laila. He recommended treating her with more respect and avoiding the restraints imposed on the other captive women. However, he cautioned that it was necessary to maintain vigilance and, if required, occasionally handcuff her to prevent any potential escape attempts from the headquarters.

Considering this advice, Omari devised a plan to both honor Laila and gingerly restrain her if the need arose. He decided to organize a bid for the acquisition of exquisite bracelets or bangles, intending to present them as gifts to impress her. This way, he hoped to create a sense of honor and provide a means to handcuff her watchfully, should the situation require it.

To ensure a proper fit on the wrist, the bracelets were designed to be flexible, featuring a locking jack mechanism. Additionally, the bracelets were equipped with lock and key latches. One of the bracelets had a hole where the lock could be inserted, while the other bracelet had a key latch to secure it. This design allowed the bracelets to serve a dual purpose, functioning both as decorative accessories and as handcuffs if the need arose.

Once the bracelet was placed on the wrist, it could not be removed without the accompanying keys or the use of a cutting machine. Further, this design ensured that the bracelets provided a secure means of restraint as handcuffs with an additional locking system, should it become necessary.

Omari dispatched his trusted men to Dubai, a city renowned for its gold market, with the task of procuring custom-made, regal-looking gold bracelets adorned with diamonds, precisely as he had envisioned. The intent was to acquire bracelets that exuded a sense of royalty and beauty, aligning with Omari's desires. These exquisite bracelets were specially crafted to meet Omari's demands.

Finally, on the auspicious occasion of Eid, a marked celebration in the Muslim calendar, Omari presented the most expensive bracelet to Laila as a heartfelt gift. The intention behind this gesture was to demonstrate his admiration and affection for her and to express his desire to honor and impress her.

Laila was summoned to make an appearance before the entire Royal court, where she was expected to be attired in a full-body hijab. The kazi, following the complete Islamic ritual, presented the bracelets to her. Other women in attendance offered their assistance, supporting the flexible sections of the bracelets as they helped Laila wear them on both wrists. They proceeded to lock the individual bracelet's locking jacks, ensuring they were securely fastened, and handed the key to Omari.

During the same ceremony, Laila was also bestowed with several unique and luxurious full-body cover hijabs, specially designed to set her apart from the other women. This was to symbolize her status as a Royal princess and the future queen. By wearing the golden bracelets and the distinctive Royal hijab, Laila became an exceptional figure among all the women in the Royal palace. Wherever she went, people bestowed honor upon her and treated her with utmost respect, recognizing her as a Royal princess.

Winning Laila's heart became equally significant to Omari as his pursuit of a radical war against India. She had become a matter of great pride and prestige for him, prompting him to be resolute in his determination to win her affection.

Although the golden bracelets had locks and key latches that could have been used as handcuffs, Laila never violated the laws and regulations of the terror camp. As a result, her hands were never subjected to being handcuffed. Laila understood the severe consequences associated with attempting to escape from the camp. She was fully aware that survival on her own would be challenging and that the terrorists would likely capture and execute her as a punishment for her disobedience. Thus, Laila exercised caution and refrained from taking such risks.

16. JK Joined a Terror Group & Crossed the Border

One day, JK received disheartening news that the Indian government had made an unsuccessful attempt to retrieve Laila by agreeing to release Omari. Tragically, during the exchange, Omari managed to seize Laila once again and used her as a shield to evade the Indian military, successfully crossing the border and taking her with him to Pakistan.

Upon hearing this devastating outcome, JK returned to his military camp and confronted the higher officials, seeking accountability for the failure of the mission he had warned them about. However, they denied responsibility, stating that they were not involved in the exchange operation. Frustrated and disillusioned, JK made the difficult decision to resign from the Indian army for personal reasons, feeling a deep sense of disappointment and defeat.

After resigning from his army position, JK made a final visit to Sanam. During their meeting, he learned the joyous news that she was pregnant. Overwhelmed with happiness and excitement, he saw this as a guiding light of hope for her future. Despite his sadness at not being able to fulfill his promise of eliminating Omari, he assured Sanam that his life remained dedicated to serving their motherland, India. Although he had departed from the military, he vowed to fulfill his duty of bringing Omari to justice and avenging Tejas's sacrifice. JK conveyed to Sanam that this visit marked their final meeting, as he was preparing to venture on his next mission.

Now, JK had three compelling reasons to seek revenge from Omari. Firstly, he desired retribution for the death of his dearest friend Tejas. Secondly, he held deep resentment toward Omari for kidnapping Laila, the love of his life. Lastly, JK felt a sense of outrage at the insult inflicted upon his motherland, India, by Omari.

With determination to achieve his objectives, JK resolved to cross the border into Pakistan. He formulated a plan to join a militant camp, utilizing it as a means to cross the border covertly, and ultimately confront Omari directly. JK was prepared to take whatever actions were necessary to fulfill his quest for revenge.

JK made his way back to his sister's village, where she resided after her marriage. His sister had kept his whereabouts a secret, ensuring that nobody inquired about him. When neighbors inquired about JK, she informed them that he was employed in a Muslim Gulf country, maintaining the facade to protect him.

In the valley, there was a strong aversion to joining the Indian army. The community enforced a social, cultural, educational, and financial boycott against families with members serving in the military. Furthermore, militants subjected these families to torture within the valley. These circumstances made it crucial for JK's sister to conceal his true intentions and ensure his safety by portraying him as being away in a distant country.

After returning to the village, JK became increasingly active and developed close relationships with the youth involved in jihadi agitations against India. Through his efforts, he successfully gained the trust and support of local jihadists, who facilitated his recruitment into a terrorist camp. The jihadi movement was in full swing and demanded a large influx of recruits. Consequently, the terrorist groups bypassed proper background checks and screening procedures in their haste to acquire new members.

With the assistance of the locals, JK easily secured a place within the terror camp and began preparations to cross into PoK for intensive training. The training aimed to equip the recruits with the necessary skills to carry out acts of terrorism upon their return to the Indian side of the valley. The ultimate goal was to outbreak heinous acts of violence and destabilize the region.

Alongside the other newly recruited terrorists, JK took a treacherous journey under the cloak of darkness, intending to cross the border into PoK. However, their plans were thwarted when the Indian army apprehended them on the Indian side of the border. Led by top commander Pitambar, the army successfully captured all individuals involved.

In a harsh and freezing environment, the captured youths were stripped and paraded on the snowy hills. As the light illuminated JK's face, Pitambar recognized him, triggering a flood of memories from their past conversations and arguments regarding Tejas and Omari. Pitambar's mind briefly drifted into the past.

Observing Pitambar's recognition, JK grew apprehensive, fearing that Pitambar might seek revenge for their heated arguments and rebel against him. However, Pitambar came to realize his mistake of allowing Omari to escape and not seizing the golden opportunity to eliminate him when he had the chance.

Pitambar also recalled how JK had once challenged him, asserting that even if Omari managed to flee to Pakistan, JK would cross the border. He would track him down, and bring him to justice by terminating him. Understanding JK's plan to join the jihadi youth and cross the border into PoK, Pitambar decided to let him proceed with his mission.

Pitambar, displaying strong leadership, took a decisive stand and issued a clear and authoritative order to his team. He commanded them to release the local youths, recognizing that they were not terrorists but ordinary laborers returning home. Pitambar carefully ensured that neither the army nor the local youth were aware of his actions. He carefully stepped back and silently signaled to JK, expressing his apology and agreement with JK's mission to go to PoK.

In a gesture of respect, Pitambar saluted JK for his undertaking to seek justice for Tejas, Laila, and all of India. Understanding the graveness of JK's mission, Pitambar acknowledged the importance of what he was about to do. Finally, the military personnel departed in a different direction after advising the local boys not to engage in late-night travel in the future.

After some time, the boys successfully crossed the border into PoK using a small canal as their passage. Upon arrival, they were greeted by their pre-arranged terrorist guide, who accompanied them to the designated local terrorist training camp. Once at the camp, the boys had to undergo certain formalities and procedures before being officially admitted into the training schedule of the terrorist camp.

JK crossed the border with a clear mission in mind. Firstly, his objective was to locate Laila and dig out the whereabouts of Omari. Secondly, he aimed to ensure the safe return of Laila to her home in J&K. Finally, JK was determined to seek justice by eliminating Omari and dismantling his militant base. His motivation for these actions originated from the desire to avenge Tejas, his dearest friend. Also, he wanted to protect Laila, the love of his life, and seek justice for his motherland, India.

JK was strongly convinced that he would eventually locate Omari. As the prominent figure and leader of the militants, tracing Omari's hideout in PoK was expected to be relatively straightforward. However, JK was uncertain about finding Laila with the same ease. There was a lingering doubt in his mind, questioning whether she was still alive. He feared that the militants might have already executed her, given the reports of violence, torture, rape, and the mistreatment of innocent girls and women by Muslim radicalists.

Despite these apprehensions, JK maintained an optimistic outlook. He was a devout believer in God and held a deep affection for Laila. Whenever negative thoughts clouded his mind, he turned to prayer, seeking divine protection and well-being for her.

In moments of loneliness, he would immerse himself in the evanescent memories of his friendship with Tejas. Eventually, he sought solace in the comforting presence of Laila, finding peace in her embrace. Laila's captivating charm, innocence, and beauty never failed to mesmerize him. Those precious moments served as a source of rejuvenation for his spirit and instilled in him the determination to fight for their sake.

Whenever JK touched Laila's headscarf, it felt as though her presence enveloped him once again. He could almost sense her gentle touch and warm breath, transporting him back to the apple orchard where she had tied her headscarf around his wounded arm when he was injured. In those moments, a surge of excitement and renewed energy empowered him to face any challenges that lay ahead, driven by his love and devotion for Laila.

JK firmly believed in the purity and resilience of Laila's soul. He held the conviction that no evil forces could harm such a remarkable and virtuous spirit. He trusted that good souls remain close to the heart of God, and God, in turn, always shields them. These positive thoughts were a constant source of courage and strength, energizing JK to overcome any obstacles he encountered.

In JK's life, four precious treasures held immense weightiness: his mother's blessings, his friendship with Tejas, his deep affection for the nation, and his love for Laila. These treasures collectively electrified his zest to serve the nation, seek justice for his friend's untimely demise, guard national interests, and ensure Laila's safe return to India. They held immense humanitarian, national, and personal meaning for JK, bringing him a sense of satisfaction.

Upon crossing the border, JK's primary objective was to locate Laila. However, he faced uncertainty about how to find her amidst his assigned rigorous training in the camp. The demanding nature of the training left him with little time to dedicate to his search. While his thoughts were incessantly occupied by the desire to find both Laila and Omari, the majority of his time was consumed by the demanding terrorist training he underwent.

Being in PoK, a foreign and unfamiliar place to him, further complicated his search for Laila. The camp's strict regulations restricted his freedom to venture outside, making it increasingly challenging for him to locate her. The conditions of his training and restricted access to the outside world posed great challenges in his mission to reunite with Laila.

17. JK's Stay in PoK; Finding Laila & the Terror Boss

In the terrorist training camp, the newly recruited individuals were provided with information regarding a competition. This contest aimed to identify the top two trainees based on their performance. The selection process required each of the numerous terrorist training camps scattered across PoK to nominate their top two best-performing trainees. These selected trainees would then be sent to the headquarters in Muzaffarabad for advanced training.

Through conversations with fellow trainees, JK obtained exclusive information about the hideout of the terror boss, Omari, situated at the headquarters. It was revealed that Omari held a position of authority, overseeing and coordinating militant activities throughout PoK and the Indian side of the valley from that central location.

During a conversation between two trainers, JK learned about Omari's *mashuka* (sweetheart). The trainers gossiped about how Omari had brought a beautiful and innocent girl with him from the Indian side. They shared that initially, Omari had subjected her to torture, but over time, he developed feelings for her. It was mentioned that when she rejected his marriage proposal, Omari vowed to impress her, hoping that she would eventually propose to him herself for marriage.

JK had doubts about whether the girl they were discussing was truly Laila. He could not believe the rumors, as he knew Laila's strength of character and her determination. He believed that Laila would choose to sacrifice her own life rather than bow down to the force of the militants. However, JK could not gain a victory over his fear of the forceful nature of Muslim radicals. He was apprehensive that they might employ wicked tactics, such as rape and coercion to enforce submission.

JK decided to travel to the headquarters with the hope of finding Omari and his *mashuka*. He aspired to get closer to Omari, with the anticipation of possibly locating Laila in the process. Even if Laila was not present, JK was determined to capture Omari, viewing him as his ultimate target. Additionally, being at the headquarters could potentially provide him with valuable information about Laila's whereabouts.

Focusing his efforts, JK dedicated himself to becoming one of the top two trainees in his camp. Securing a place among the best-performing trainees would grant him admission to the headquarters. He believed it would be instrumental in finding Omari and, potentially, discovering Laila as well.

JK, being the best and most skilled Indian soldier, had exceptional training and capabilities. However, he purposely concealed his true abilities during the competitions, not wanting to draw attention to his exceptional skills. Instead, he maintained a consistent performance by finishing within the top five positions in all competitions. Despite intentionally holding back, JK's competence enabled him to qualify for entry into the headquarters by securing the second position overall.

The allocation of future missions within the training camp depended on the initial performance of the trainees. The top two performers from each camp were selected to be assigned to the terrorist headquarters, where they would undertake a classified and highly secretive mission. PoK had numerous small training camps spread across its territory. The location of the headquarters was mobile, frequently shifting from one camp to another based on intelligence inputs provided by the ISI. Over the past several months, the headquarters had been situated in a secluded area in Muzaffarabad.

Omari held a prominent position at the headquarters, being considered the ruler of PoK. He had established a temporary royal palace for himself and, notably, kept Laila under his close observation. Despite his love for Laila, Omari had made a vow to marry her only after winning her heart. To ensure her safety, he assigned several women terrorists to serve as her guards. She was permitted a certain level of freedom within the boundaries set by the regulations of Omari's palace.

Laila's assigned duties in the palace revolved around working in the kitchen and assisting other women cooks. She was obligated to stay in the vicinity of Omari whenever he returned to his shelter for rest after his demanding schedule. The intention behind this arrangement was to develop a sense of closeness and, potentially, ignite love in Laila's heart for Omari. She was tasked with attending to Omari's needs during these moments.

While Omari generally treated Laila with respect, there were occasions when he insisted on being closer to her, which she firmly rejected. During those moments, he would confront her, questioning, "How long will it take you to be convinced? Just go away now but one day you will bring yourself under my shoulder."

In response, Laila, filled with anguish, taunted him, emphasizing the impossibility of winning someone's heart against their wishes. She remarked, "You can kidnap someone by force. But you cannot win someone's heart against one's wish." With those poignant words, she vanished from sight.

JK, along with the other chosen recruits from various field camps, arrived at the main base camp headquarters in Muzaffarabad. His demeanor and appearance had undergone a complete transformation. Uncertain if Laila would recognize him, he frequently wore the headscarf on his wrist. JK hoped that she would catch sight of it and recognize her headscarf, even from a distance.

During his time in the Indian army, JK maintained a clean-shaven look and exuded a handsome appearance. However, in the terrorist camp, he adopted a jihadi appearance, completely altering his exterior and attire. He grew out a mullah's beard, mustache, and hair. This new guise made it challenging for individuals who knew him during his military service to recognize him within the militant camp.

On the first day at the headquarters, all the new recruits participated in a formal interaction with the personnel for the next level of training and planning. The session was inaugurated by Omari, the leader of the terrorists. JK stood among the recruits in the back row, and upon catching sight of Omari, he was momentarily transported back in time.

Images of Tejas skiing downhill, carrying Omari on his back, flooded JK's mind. He vividly remembered how he had rescued an unconscious Omari from his fallen friend's embrace and handed him over to other army personnel for transport. He recalled his burning desire for revenge, wanting to kill Omari during that very moment during transportation. JK also recalled the injection of sedatives administered by Pitambar, causing him to lose consciousness. Taking a deep breath, JK reflected on these memories.

His colleagues noticed his rapid breathing and offered assistance. They were concerned that he might not be feeling well. However, JK managed to regain control of his emotions, behaving as though nothing had occurred. Deep inside, he felt immense satisfaction, realizing that he had successfully found Omari. JK believed that he had already secured half of the battle by locating him. From that point onwards, he embraced a sense of happiness and contentment.

Whenever JK felt a sense of happiness, he would share his witty jokes, bringing laughter to those around him. His humor quickly gained popularity, and he became known for his ability to entertain with his wisecracks. People would specifically seek him out in the main camp, eagerly demanding rib-ticklers from him. In no time, news of his comedic talent reached the ears of Omari.

Impressed by the reputation JK had gained, Omari extended an invitation to a small gathering, where JK was asked to share his jokes. As time went on, Omari himself found amusement in JK's jokes and requested that he join him occasionally for more laughs. The arrival of the newly recruited trainees at the headquarters brought about positive changes in Omari's life, and JK played a chief role in this transformation. Among the new recruits, JK stood out as someone who brought a sense of positivity to the camp, always making an effort to impress Omari with his jokes and overall demeanor.

One day, a colleague in Omari's court approached JK, curious about why he always wore a beautiful headscarf on his wrist. JK's eyes lit up with enthusiasm as he began recounting the incident behind it. Unbeknownst to him, Laila was observing the activities outside from a nearby room, her gaze fixed on the window. As her eyes fell upon the headscarf, a sense of familiarity washed over her. It was the very same headscarf she had once tied on JK's wrist. However, due to JK's transformed appearance and the distance between them, she could not recognize him. Intrigued by the conversation, Laila decided to pay closer attention and listen in.

JK passionately narrated the incident, recounting how he had fallen from an apple tree and how his sweetheart had come to his aid, applying medication and tying her headscarf around his injured arm to stem the bleeding. With pride, he raised his wrist, bringing the scarf closer to his chest, emphasizing that it was the very same scarf he held dear. His colleague playfully teased him, suggesting what would happen if someone were to steal the scarf. In a heartfelt tone, JK responded, "I would die without it, as this headscarf holds the only precious memory left in my life."

Continuing the teasing, his colleague remarked, "Brother, it seems like you are deeply in love with her."

With genuine acceptance, JK replied, "Indeed, yes!"

Hearing the conversation, Laila's heart filled with joy as she recognized JK's voice. She became certain that it was indeed him, and her happiness soared, knowing that he loved her deeply enough to venture across the border for her sake. However, a sense of fear enveloped her as she realized the danger surrounding them within the headquarters. She understood that any act of assistance or seeking favors from JK could potentially put both of their lives at risk.

With caution and wisdom, Laila decided to bide her time and wait for the opportune moment to reveal herself to JK. She longed for him to recognize her, and believed that the right moment would come when they could safely reconnect without endangering their lives. Until then, she would remain patient and await the perfect opportunity for their paths to cross once again.

One fine morning, Laila overheard Omari lavishing praise upon her, expressing the depth of his love. Even as he uttered these words, Omari was fully cognizant of Laila's presence in an adjacent room, aware that his declaration of affection reached her ears.

During a late evening gathering, Omari graciously extended an invitation to all the new recruits, welcoming them to his full court for an engaging event filled with humor and conversation. This special event was open to all at the headquarters, and the women attendees followed the rule of wearing a full hijab for privacy.

As JK skillfully shared his comedic talents, the audience, including Omari and Laila, found themselves thoroughly entertained and appreciative of his wit and humor. The atmosphere was enlivened by the joyful laughter that echoed throughout the court. Omari took notice of Laila's genuine enjoyment of JK's jokes, which was a rare sight, as she had seldom expressed such positivity before. Witnessing Laila's newfound happiness, Omari began to believe that JK's presence was bringing a stroke of good luck to his surroundings.

However, as Laila was enwrapped in a hijab, JK could not identify her. Within a remarkably brief span, JK had managed to earn the favor and trust of Omari, becoming his esteemed and cherished companion. However, unbeknownst to Omari, an intricate connection was blossoming between JK and Laila, a secret that remained concealed from his watchful gaze.

Upon the realization that JK was present within the headquarters, Laila's demeanor underwent a remarkable transformation. She shed her previous aloofness, displaying newfound cooperation and a cheerful attitude. Omari, observing this change in her behavior, could not help but feel a surge of contentment. He attributed Laila's altered disposition to the arrival of the new recruit, JK, whom he believed to be a harbinger of good fortune. In Omari's eyes, it seemed that everything was aligning favorably for him.

Caught in the enchantment of his daydreams, Omari envisioned a future where Laila would openly confess her love for him, tendering a proposal of marriage. His heart soared with the anticipation of a perfect union, and he basked in the belief that he had found himself in a win-win situation in all aspects. Meanwhile, news of a successful militant operation across the border reached him. This strengthened his sense of accomplishment and reinforcing his belief that destiny was on his side.

JK had an encounter with the main Royal lady, adorned in a dignified hijab. Her laughter and voice bore an uncanny resemblance to Laila, sparking a flicker of doubt within JK's heart. However, bound by the stringent security protocols in place, he hesitated to approach her directly and inquire about her true identity. The longing to confirm whether it was indeed Laila hidden beneath the veil intensified, scaling up his curiosity and anxiety.

Yet circumstances conspired against JK, denying him the opportune moment to seek the truth and dispel his doubts. The effort to know the true person behind the hijab, whose laughter and voice reflected Laila's essence, remained a perplexing puzzle. It left JK craving for answers and assurance.

After a successful militant operation across the border, Omari rolled out a regal celebration. A group of dancers and singers, predominantly donning hijabs, were summoned to grace the occasion with their performances. In their midst, a few English girls stood out, their heads bare without the customary hijab. Omari, accompanied by esteemed guests, occupied a central position as the festivities commenced. Given that one of his regular guards was unwell, Omari designated JK as his temporary personal security detail and invited him to sit nearby. With anticipation building, the performers took to the stage, ready to captivate the audience with their artistic talents.

The melodious voice resonated from the woman adorned in a hijab, as she began to sing, "*Laila Mai Aisi….*"

The enchanting melody reverberated in the ears of both JK and Omari. JK, recognizing the voice, felt an overwhelming sense of joy, yet restrained his emotions for security reasons. Meanwhile, Omari was taken aback by the familiar sound, finding it hard to believe that it was Laila's voice.

Acting swiftly, Omari rose from his seat and approached the woman in the hijab who was singing. With a sudden movement, he lifted her hijab, revealing Laila beneath. The sight of Laila singing left Omari astonished. In that momentary exchange, JK caught a glimpse of her face, and their eyes met briefly, igniting a spark of recognition between them. Laila lifted her hand, showcasing the royal gold bracelet adorning her wrist, serving as a distinctive identifier whenever she wore the hijab. This triggered JK's memory, aligning with the information shared by a colleague regarding the royal bracelet belonging to Omari's *mashuka*. Omari was elated to witness Laila's captivating performance, as she sang a mesmerizing song that praised him. Throughout the performance, Laila intermittently wore a partial hijab, covering only her nose and mouth, adhering to the strict guidelines for women's attire.

LAILA MAI AISI
(*Voice*: Ms. Alka Yagnik)

Laila mai aisi hui teri deewani, is deewangi ki hai ajab kahani
is deewangi ki hai ghazab kahani
laila mai aisi hui teri deewani, is deewangi ki hai ajab kahani
is deewangi ki hai ghazab kahani

Teri har baat humko lagti hai pyari
teri har baat humko lagti hai pyari, teri baat mein meri duniya hai saari
is deewangi ki hai ajab kahani

Har baat sun li ab to teri hi zubani
har baat sun li ab to teri hi zubani, teri baat pe hi to Laila hai deewani
is deewangi ki hai ghazab kahani

Laila mai aisi hui teri deewani, is deewangi ki hai ajab kahani
is deewangi ki hai ghazab kahani

Teri mast adaon pe mai dil haari
teri mast adaon pe mai dil haari, tere deedar se mai hui mastani
is deewangi ki hai ajab kahani

Rab se to har pal maine mannat hai mangi
rab se to har pal maine mannat hai mangi, puri kab hogi apani adhuri kahani
is deewangi ki hai ghazab kahani

Laila mai aisi hui teri deewani, is deewangi ki hai ajab kahani
is deewangi ki hai ghazab kahani

Omari, enveloped in a cloud of delusion, found himself overjoyed, as he believed the beautiful song being sung was dedicated to him. The melody resonated deep within his soul, and he could not help but feel an overwhelming sense of pride. In his mind, Laila's alluring voice was an affirmation of her love for him.

Unbeknownst to Omari, Laila's true intentions lay elsewhere. She had come to realize JK's unremitting love for her and his determination to rescue her from the clutches of Omari and bring her back to safety. As Laila sang, she subtly conveyed her message to JK through her body language and eye contact. It was a silent reassurance, a promise of unity and hope.

Meanwhile, JK, ever observant and quick-witted, understood Laila's signals. He saw through the illusions woven by Omari's misinterpretation of the song. He knew that Laila's heart belonged to him and that she sang for him, not Omari. Their connection was stronger than ever, solidified in that brief moment when their eyes met.

In Omari's blissful ignorance, he ordered a relaxation of security measures around Laila. Convinced of her love and compliance, he envisioned their forthcoming nuptials. However, JK saw this as an opportunity, a chance to strike when the time was right. With both Omari and Laila now within reach, JK began to meticulously plan his next move, knowing that their fate hung in the balance.

18. JK Saved Laila

In the wake of an epoch-making engagement, Omari and his main team departed the headquarters, leaving behind an opportune void. Recognizing the favorable circumstances, Laila seized the moment to execute their daring plan. With utmost heedfulness, she passed a full-body hijab, and a meticulously crafted letter to JK during a covert encounter at the palace, where he had arrived to collect an assignment.

Aware of the risks, JK followed the instructions outlined in the letter. With the full-body hijab carefully draped over him, JK transformed into a disguised figure, concealing his true identity from prying eyes. The clever camouflage allowed him to blend seamlessly among the women in the palace, his presence unquestioned. Laila had informed the guards that a helper woman was expected, further aiding in their clandestine plan.

In the secluded space where Laila eagerly awaited his arrival, JK stepped forward, his disguised presence shrouded in the full-body hijab. Their reunion was a moment of acute specialness, as their destinies converged under the veil of secrecy. Engaging in a heartfelt and extensive conversation, they scrupulously planned their escape from the confines of the terrorist camp.

JK had crucial information regarding the impending dispatch of a suicide squad by the headquarters, with the specific objective of assassinating the Indian Prime Minister on Indian soil. Driven by a resolute determination, JK set his sights on being selected as the primary human bomb for this perilous mission. To achieve this, he invested unhesitating effort into establishing himself as Omari's most trusted and indispensable confidant. By cultivating an unshakeable bond with Omari, JK aimed to secure his endorsement for the assignment.

Simultaneously, JK engaged in discreet discussions with Laila to map out their escape. They strategically synchronized their exit strategy with the precise moment when JK would be deployed across the border for the high-stakes suicide mission. Aware of the inherent dangers in their shared mission, JK and Laila worked together to plan a flawless escape. They zeroed in on ways to sidestep detection and execute their plan successfully.

Omari was in search of an individual who had trustworthiness and courage beyond doubt to undertake the crucial suicide mission in India. The militants placed great importance on selecting someone they could wholeheartedly rely on to accomplish the mission, as it held immense sanctity for them. They preached that this sacred opportunity was granted by Allah solely to individuals who held a special place in His heart. Calling them to undertake the suicide mission, Allah displayed His boundless affection for them. This promised a heavenly abode and the privilege of staying close to Him as a reward for their noble mission.

At the same time, JK strategically aimed to impress the terrorists, notably Omari, by displaying his exceptional competence and outperforming his peers for the suicide mission. With his stupendous efforts, JK instilled confidence in himself that Omari would ultimately choose him for the mission. After deliberating the matter with his counselors, Omari concluded that JK was the most suitable candidate and officially selected him for the mission.

Prior to the announcement of his selection for the suicide mission, JK had already formulated an intricate plan. He outlined the steps he would take to facilitate Laila's escape from the headquarters. JK strategized the means by which he would aid her in crossing the border safely. He also crafted the final phase of his plan, visualizing his comeback to the headquarters. The ultimate step included dismantling the organization and eradicating Omari and the other terrorists.

JK's detailed plan encompassed the different stages of their escape and retribution. He carefully considered the logistics, potential obstacles, and contingencies to ensure the success of each step. By methodically plotting their getaway and subsequent assault on the headquarters, JK aimed to secure both Laila's freedom and the eradication of the terrorist organization, culminating in the downfall of Omari and his cohorts.

The militants strategically selected August 16 as a symbolic date, coinciding with Pakistan's Independence Day on August 14 and

India's Independence Day on August 15. They intended to use August 16 as a day to mark the "independence" of PoK. Their plan was to carry out the assassination of the Indian Prime Minister on this date, symbolically associating it with the independence of PoK.

By targeting the Indian Prime Minister on August 16, the militants sought to commemorate this day and use it as a catalyst to escalate their struggle for the liberation of Indian-occupied Kashmir. Their primary goal was to commemorate the real Independence Day on the same date the following year. This was their trophy in their struggle for freedom. The choice of August 16 held deep symbolic meaning for the militants, as they aimed to use it as a rallying point to inspire and mobilize support for their cause.

Anticipating the news of the Indian Prime Minister's assassination on the morning of August 16, the militants had arranged for a grand celebration at their headquarters in Muzaffarabad later in the afternoon. The event was planned to coincide with their symbolic independence day for PoK. Additionally, they had invited Mualana Omar, the chief of the Taliban, to partake in the momentous occasion, further elevating its significance.

The celebration was expected to attract a large gathering, including thousands of militants, ISI agents, and Pakistani army personnel. Omari, as the organizer, had smartly planned and coordinated the event, aiming to unite and rally support for their cause in PoK. The festivities were meant to serve as a proxy Independence Day celebration, bringing together like-minded individuals who shared the vision of liberating Indian-occupied Kashmir.

The guests had arrangements to spend the night in nearby villages on August 15, as part of the planned event. This gathering served a twofold purpose: first, to celebrate the successful assassination of the Indian Prime Minister. Second, to establish a foundation day for the independence of Indian-occupied Kashmir. The ultimate goal was to consolidate the integration of the Indian Occupied Kashmir into the territory of PoK.

In India, it had become customary for the Prime Minister to visit the Army headquarters in Kashmir on the morning of August 16, the day following Independence Day. This visit served as a way to express support, encouragement, and solidarity toward the Indian Army. The Defense Minister held the second-highest popularity rank and was positioned as the potential successor to the Prime Minister. However, the government's return to power in the upcoming general election seemed unlikely.

Under these circumstances, the Defense Minister entered into a secret pact with a terror group from PoK to eliminate the current Prime Minister at the Army headquarters in Srinagar. The objective was to clear the path for the Defense Minister to assume the role of Prime Minister at an earlier time than originally expected.

The choice of the Army headquarters in Srinagar as the location for the assassination was influenced by its convenience for both the terrorists and the Defense Minister. The geographical proximity made it accessible for the terrorists. Whereas, the presence of the Army provided cover and a favorable environment for the minister. Additionally, the Defense Minister had the support of trusted Army officers who were willing to take action in his favor.

This clandestine deal aimed to grant access and ensure cover for the terrorist suicide squad during the Prime Minister's usual visit to the Army headquarters in Srinagar on August 16.

After Omari's announcement, JK was designated as the lead suicide operative within the squad. He was tasked with assassinating the Indian Prime Minister during his visit to Kashmir on August 16. With his selection confirmed, JK's intensive training for the mission commenced.

Simultaneously, JK was also working covertly on his own mission. He devised plans to ensure the safe escape of Laila from the militant headquarters. Additionally, JK aimed to eliminate Omari and his team, dismantling their operation in PoK. Furthermore, he strategized to destroy the substantial stockpile of arms and ammunition within the headquarters. The sole aim was to disrupt the terror network that operated in PoK against India.

With a dual agenda in mind, JK prepared himself both mentally and physically for his role as the main human bomb while plotting the execution of his personal mission. His actions were driven by the determination to ensure Laila's freedom, neutralize the threat posed by Omari and his group, and destabilize the terrorist network operating in PoK.

Quietly and covertly, JK took the initiative to connect all the stockpiled arms and ammunition within the headquarters to his remote control system before setting sail on the suicide mission. In a strategic move, he also planted landmines and other destructive devices throughout the headquarters and the designated area for the anticipated Independence Day gathering. These explosives were precisely connected to the same remote control system.

JK's objective was clear: to completely demolish the terrorist camp, leaving no trace of its existence. By linking the armaments and the strategically placed explosives to his remote control, JK sought to ensure maximum destruction.

In the late evening of August 15, JK received assistance in donning the complete suicide bomb vest, effectively turning him into a human bomb for the impending mission. Alongside four other terrorists, he was transported in a vehicle toward the border, taking advantage of the cover provided by the night darkness. They intended to enter the Indian side of Kashmir, preparing for the mission scheduled for the following morning.

Upon arrival at the Indian side, the terrorists had pre-arranged logistical support to ensure JK's timely arrival in Srinagar for the mission. These arrangements were made to facilitate their operations and assist in the execution of their plan. The specific details and nature of this groundwork was known only to the terrorists involved, ensuring a degree of confidentiality throughout their mission.

After leaving the headquarters, JK sought an opportune moment to execute his initial plan. Finding a secluded location, he took decisive action and eliminated all the terrorists accompanying him. With the threat neutralized, JK took control of the vehicle and proceeded to the predetermined location to pick up Laila. This calculated move ensured their reunion and set their escape plan into motion.

Laila managed to administer a sedative to everyone within the headquarters by discreetly adding it to the food served during dinner. Once she ensured that everyone was incapacitated, Laila slipped out of the headquarters unnoticed. Meanwhile, JK, following their pre-arranged plan, picked her up from the designated location.

Together, JK and Laila set forth on an expedition toward the Indian border near Muzaffarabad. At this point, Laila remained unaware of JK's additional plan and was under the impression that JK would simply accompany her in crossing the border into India. Their ultimate destination and the true nature of JK's intentions were yet to be revealed to Laila.

When JK picked up Laila to drive toward the border, her heart brimmed with happiness, feeling like a liberated bird soaring into the vast sky. The sense of freedom engulfed her, but the true source of her joy was being in the company of JK, the person she had recently fallen in love with. The mere hour spent together on their journey felt like a lifetime to Laila, a time of unparalleled bliss that she had never experienced before. Similarly, JK cherished every moment beside the girl he loved, grateful for their togetherness.

However, amidst their happiness, JK's mind remained focused on the subsequent course of action after safely guiding Laila to the Indian border. He skillfully concealed any indications of concern or anxiety, presenting a facade of contentment to keep Laila in the dark about his plan to backtrack to the headquarters. Laila relished every second of the journey toward the border, feeling as if she had already lived a complete life with JK. She eagerly planned numerous adventures and dreams to be fulfilled alongside JK once they returned to India. Unbeknownst to her, JK harbored his own backstairs plan, awaiting execution at the headquarters.

JK and Laila reached the border village of Teetwal, which was divided by the LOC between India and Pakistan. The village was split by the LOC, with the Kishanganga River, known as the Neelum River on the Pakistani side, acting as the dividing line between the two countries. As a result, half of the village belonged to India, while the other half fell within Pakistan. This division occurred during the establishment of the LOC between India and Pakistan.

The Pakistani side of the village was called Chilhana and was part of the Neelum Valley in Muzaffarabad, PoK. Although geographically, the other side belonged to PoK, in their hearts, the people on that side were more aligned toward India. Initially, the two sides of the village were connected by a narrow bridge. However, due to deteriorating relations between India and Pakistan, the bridge was closed, and both nations deployed heavy security forces on their respective sides of the border. The villagers had relatives and connections on both sides, further highlighting the complexities and interwoven relationships between the two communities divided by political boundaries.

JK had distant relatives residing in Chilhana, the PoK side of the village. Utilizing the cover of darkness, JK and Laila sought refuge in his relatives' home. Gaining their trust, JK shared his stories and sought their assistance. His relatives, who held a stronger alignment toward India, agreed to help him and Laila in the tragic situation.

To ensure a seamless border crossing without arousing suspicions, JK instructed Laila to replace her royal hijab with a simple dress provided by their relatives. This would help avoid any unnecessary attention during their wayfaring.

Laila had cleverly copied the key pattern of the bracelet onto a bar of soap, having retrieved the original key from Omari's secret hiding place as part of their plan. JK asked Laila for the soap sample with the key imprint, as he planned to make duplicate keys to remove the bracelet from her wrist and place it on his own. He instructed his relative to assist in creating a duplicate key to remove the bracelet from Laila's wrist. With the assistance of his relatives, a duplicate key was successfully crafted, enabling them to remove the bracelet from Laila's wrist as planned.

Laila observed JK as he shaved his beard, mustache, and even the hair on his hands. Laila was overjoyed to see JK's original appearance, exactly as she had first seen him when he visited her at her house. However, she was taken aback by the sight of him shaving the hair on his hands. Unbeknownst to her, JK was doing so to match the appearance of a woman's hand.

After shaving, JK proceeded to put on the royal full-body hijab and the bracelet that Laila had previously taken off. He intended to avoid raising any suspicions when he entered the headquarters disguised as Laila. JK took great care to ensure his appearance perfectly matched Laila's attire and demeanor. He eliminated any doubts or questions that might arise when he entered the headquarters in her royal attire and with her bracelet. His attention to detail was crucial to maintaining the authenticity of the disguise.

Eventually, Laila's patience reached its limit, and she confronted JK about his mysterious behavior and hidden intentions. Urging him repeatedly, she demanded an explanation. Finally, JK revealed the truth to her, explaining that while she would be returning to India, he was obligated to go back to the militant headquarters.

Laila was devastated upon discovering that JK would be returning to the headquarters after assisting her in crossing the border. The revelation of this new twist in their plan deeply saddened her. The mere thought of being separated from him was unbearable, and she poured out her heart, confessing her deep love for him. Laila expressed that her love for JK surpassed anything else in her life and declared that she could not imagine living without him. Believing that they were finally free and safe, Laila could not comprehend why JK would willingly choose to go back to the oppressive world of terrorism.

Laila suggested with hope in her voice, "We can easily run away from this place."

"Please try to understand me," JK answered while preparing to leave.

Her heart yearned for them to start a new life together. "We can go to the south part of India or even to a Western country where the terrorists will not find us. Please, let's try to understand each other," she implored emotionally, desperately wanting JK to reconsider.

With tears streaming down his face, JK earnestly tried to convey his reasons for his return. He spoke in a voice filled with emotion, sharing with Laila that his very existence was owed to Tejas, who valiantly sacrificed his own life to save JK. The revelation of Tejas' death came as a shock to Laila, as she too had a friendly bond with him. Memories of the past flooded her mind, momentarily transporting her to the times when Tejas and JK used to visit her home.

JK continued, his voice trembling with deep sorrow, as he recounted his dearest friend, Tejas, had taken his final breath in his arms, urging him to bring Omari to justice. The weight of Tejas' sacrifice and the gift of life he bestowed upon JK were forever etched in his memory. How could JK ever forget the selflessness and courage displayed by Tejas, who had saved his life? The deep-seated impact of

Tejas' sacrifice and his dying wish to seek justice resonated deeply within JK's heart.

JK continued to express his deep love for Laila, emphasizing that she meant more to him than anything else. However, he explained that in this life, he was bound by his marriage to his duty toward the nation. Tearfully, he requested Laila to bid him farewell with joy and support for his crucial and sacred mission.

Understanding the gravity of his chosen path, JK urged Laila not to wait for him, as he knew the likely outcome of his mission. Nevertheless, he made a promise to her that, if by some miracle he returned safely—though he was fully aware of its impossibility—he would always be by her side. In his heart, he remained forever connected to Laila, and he vowed that if they were not destined to be together in this life, he would pray for their reunion in the next.

JK once again stressed his bona fide commitment to his national duty. He echoed fulfilling the promise he made to his dearest friend, Tejas, to bring Omari to justice. With a heavy heart, JK prepared to depart, carrying the weight of his love for Laila and the immense responsibility resting upon his shoulders.

Finally, JK entrusted Laila with a bravery medal, instructing her that when she received news of Omari's death, she should pass the medal to Tejas's wife in Srinagar. It was Sanam who would then return the medal to Tejas's grandma, symbolizing that JK, as a friend of Tejas, had fulfilled his promise of bringing Omari to justice. He requested Laila to convey his salute to grandma and the message that the bravery medal had truly inspired these martyrs to fulfill their mission of national duty and service.

JK also handed over a letter mentioning the names of the perpetrators on the Indian side and asked Laila to take it to Pitambar.

Laila's love and admiration for JK grew even stronger upon realizing the depth of his love and care for her. She understood that this was the reason he had prioritized her safety and ensured her passage to India before taking up his mission of revenge. However, the thought of losing him filled her with fear, as her feelings for him had grown deeper and she had truly fallen in love with him.

Despite her apprehensions, upon hearing JK's staunch commitment toward the nation, Laila found solace and felt immense pride in the person she loved. She knew that JK reciprocated her love and was willing to sacrifice for a greater cause. With a heavy heart, she gave him her complete support to live and die for the nation, recognizing the relevance of his national duty. Overwhelmed by emotions, she provided him the encouragement he needed to fulfill his duty.

Aware that she was going to lose her love, Laila was filled with bravery, courage, love, and affection. She placed a sacred coronation "*Raj Tilak*" mark on JK's forehead as a symbol of victory. She fervently chanted "*Jai Hind*" as she bid him farewell, expressing her heartfelt support for his mission. Departing with JK's relatives to cross the border, Laila could not help but sob, occasionally looking back with the hope that JK would change his mind and decide to accompany her to India.

JK's relative, a local resident familiar with a secret route, guided Laila in crossing the border without detection by the Indian or Pakistani army. He had made a promise to JK to ensure her safe arrival in her native place.

From the PoK side, JK carefully monitored Laila's crossing of the border, ensuring her passage through the river canal and into the safety of the Indian side. Once assured of Laila's safety, JK hurried back to the terrorist headquarters in Muzaffarabad, racing against time before anyone awoke from the sedative's effects.

As JK faded into the distance, Laila's tears began to flow uncontrollably. Memories of her time with JK ruled over her mind—the depth of his love, his selflessness in saving and sending her to India. She experienced not only love but also a deep sense of gratitude for his courage and sacrifice, risking his life to shield her from the terrorists. With heartfelt prayers, she sought the well-being and victory of JK, entrusting his fate to a higher power. Her farewell to JK was a bittersweet melody, with every note filled with the echoes of their love, leaving a lingering, heartstring-tugging symphony in his heart.

The compassionate villagers on the Indian side provided assistance and shelter to Laila, ensuring her safety. They also made arrangements for her secure transportation to her village near Srinagar, where she could finally find solace and reunite with her loved ones.

19. JK Assassinated the Terror Boss

Wearing Laila's attire and bracelet, JK returned to the headquarters, seeking to appear identical to her. He made his way to Laila's room, where he discovered a pamphlet that had been distributed throughout the camp, announcing a change in the schedule for the Proxy Independence Day celebration. The contents of the pamphlet triggered a memory of the conversation JK had with Laila during their journey to the border.

Laila had mentioned that Maulana Omar, the Taliban chief, sent a letter to Omari, urgently requesting to see his younger brother due to a severe case of pneumonia. Consequently, Omar would be unable to attend the celebration on August 16, and concerns were raised regarding his survival. This information resurfaced in JK's mind, providing him with crucial insight into the upcoming events and potential vulnerabilities within the camp.

Omari had to travel to Afghanistan to visit his ailing brother, Omar, which led to a change in plans for the proxy Independence Day celebration in PoK. In light of Omari's departure, the celebration was rescheduled to take place in the morning instead of the originally planned afternoon timing. As a result, the proxy celebration in PoK and the Indian Prime Minister's celebration with the Indian army in Srinagar were set to occur nearly simultaneously.

In the morning, several individuals in the headquarters, including Omari, were still affected by the sedative from the previous night, causing them to be disoriented and not fully alert. Meanwhile, the terrorists from other camps had taken up residence in nearby villages, preparing to join the celebration. As the guests began to assemble for the event, Laila was assigned a seat in the VIP lounge, positioned adjacent to Omari.

Disguised in Laila's attire, JK took his place at the assigned seat alongside Omari and the other guests. Remarkably, no one suspected that the person sitting there was not the real Laila. The deception remained undetected, allowing JK to blend impeccably into the gathering, poised to carry out his mission.

After a series of speeches, it was Omari's turn to address the audience and hoist the PoK flag. In the midst of one speech, JK spotted an opportune moment to initiate his mission. While Omari was engaged in a conversation with another individual, JK swiftly launched himself at him, firmly gripping his neck. Demonstrating dead set determination, JK aimed his pistol at Omari's forehead and discharged multiple bullets, each representing a beloved person or cause in his life. He confidently proclaimed, "The first for Tejas, the second for Laila, and the third for the motherland India, *Jai Hind.*"

As a result, JK's shots found their mark, instantly terminating Omari's life. Simultaneously, other terrorists present began to retaliate by opening fire on JK. Despite the incoming gunfire, JK fearlessly shouted at the attackers, declaring, "Morons, I am all yours, *Yamduta!* Let's play with fire."

The terrorists continued their relentless gunfire toward JK as he operated the remote on his belly, systematically eliminating both the militants and the buildings within the headquarters. With each press of the button, JK triggered explosions, causing chaos and devastation. Finally, in a resolute act, JK shouted, "*Jai Hind,*" and detonated the human bomb attached to his abdomen. The blast engulfed him and set off a chain reaction, igniting all the accumulated arms, ammunition, and strategically placed landmines. The resulting explosion sparked off a massive wave of destruction, obliterating everything within the headquarters. There were no survivors, and JK, in his ultimate sacrifice, became a martyr, ensuring the annihilation of the militants and their resources. Like the setting sun, the brave soldier's life dipped below the horizon, leaving the nation in the shadows of his courage.

Meanwhile, on the Indian side in Kashmir, a celebration was underway to commemorate the visit of the Indian Prime Minister. Coinciding with the destruction of the PoK headquarters, the Prime Minister had arranged for renowned singers to perform the song "*Watan Jawan Hamara...*" This was organized as a token of praise and tribute to the Indian armed forces. The unfolding events perfectly aligned with the magnitude of JK's heroic mission, creating a poignant and symbolic connection between the song and the destruction of the PoK headquarters.

WATAN JAWAN HAMARA

(*Voice*: Ms. Anuradha Paudwal & Mr. Suresh Wadkar)

Mai hun tum ho aur hum sab hain khushhal yahan
sarhad par hai koi jo hum sabki kar raha hai rakhwaliyan…

Watan jawan hamara jawano tum se hai.e.e.e
watan jawan hamara jawano tum se hai.e.e.e
watan jawan hamara jawano tum se hai.e.e.e
buland awaz ka aghaz har andaz tumhi se hai
watan jawan hamara jawano tum se hai.e.e.e
buland awaz ka aghaz har andaz tumhi se hai

Dayein bayein tham dayein bayein tham
parade tham parade tham parade tham tham tham
Ye rhythm tum se hai…
Na sardi ho na garmi ho na ho barsat ka gam
thithurti raaton pighalti dhoopon fisalti rahon
me na ab koi dum dum
jahan parte tere pawan ye kadam

Watan jawan hamara jawano tum se hai.e.e.e
buland awaz ka aghaz har andaz tumhi se hai

Jan gan man jan gan man
jay he jay he jay he jay jay jay jay he
tirange ki saan tumse hai…

Paharon dariyaon ya ho dushmanon ke sitam
door manzil kathin dagar ho, fauladi hausle
na hote kam kam
tumko karte hain hum veeron naman

Watan jawan hamara jawano tum se hai.e.e.e
buland awaz ka aghaz har andaz tumhi se hai

As the destruction unfolded at the PoK headquarters, the resonance of the explosions reached across the borders, capturing the attention of those on the Indian side. The power of the blasts and the determination behind JK's mission was felt even amidst the ongoing celebration of the Indian Prime Minister's visit.

The second part of the song, "*Watan Jawan hamara...*" echoed through the air, coinciding with the intensity and magnitude of the destruction. The lyrics honored the bravery and sacrifices of Indian soldiers, setting the scene for JK's mission to dismantle the PoK headquarters. The timing and synchronicity of the song and the mission created a profound and emotional resonance, symbolizing the indomitable spirit of the nation and the triumph over terrorism.

As the echoes of the explosions subsided, the realization of JK's sacrifice and the destruction he had caused began to sink in. His selfless act had not only eliminated the immediate threat of the militants but had also dealt a severe blow to their network in PoK. The nation mourned the loss of a brave martyr, who had given everything for the cause of justice and freedom.

It would be remembered as a defining moment in the fight against terrorism, where one individual's dedication and sacrifice left an indelible mark on the nation's history. JK's heroism would be forever etched in the hearts of the people, a symbol of the strength and resilience of the Indian spirit.

Pitambar, in an effort to rectify his past mistake and fulfill his duty to the nation, forwarded JK's letter, received from Laila, to the Prime Minister's Office. After a confidential investigation involving call detail records (CDRs) and other sources, the actual perpetrators of the plot against the Indian Prime Minister were identified, found guilty, and subsequently imprisoned in accordance with the law.

**Laila concluded her narrative by returning the bravery medal to grandma, symbolizing the cycle of inspiration and national duty. The medal, originally given by grandma to Tejas to ignite his patriotism and dedication to serving the nation, was passed on to JK as a source of motivation for his mission to bring the militants to justice. JK, fulfilling his promise to Tejas and driven by his duty to the nation, had eliminated the militant forces, sacrificing his own life in the process. Now, it was Laila's responsibility to fulfill JK's final wish by returning the medal to grandma.

As the story continued, grandma called Tejas' child to come closer, drawing the attention and support of everyone present. With some difficulty, grandma spoke to the child, expressing her joy at their presence and drawing a parallel between the child and his father, Tejas. She asked the child, "My grandchild, I am glad you came. At your age, what do you aspire to become in life?"

Gazing at the bravery medal, the child replied without hesitation, "I want to become an army man to serve my country!"

Grandma's heart filled with indescribable happiness upon hearing these words from the young child. She extended her trembling hand and gently positioned the bravery medal around the child's neck, offering her blessings, "May God bless you for upholding our family's legacy of duty, service, and sacrifice for our beloved nation. Now I can peacefully take my last breath. *Jai Hind*."

In that poignant moment, grandma's breathing became labored, and soon after, she took her final breath. The room was filled with a solemn silence as everyone mourned the loss of their beloved matriarch.

After grandma's passing, John, along with prominent figures from both the Hindu and Muslim villages, urged Sanam to assume the role left vacant due to the loss of both grandma and Masterji. Their guidance and persuasion convinced Sanam to take charge of running the village school. Whereas, Laila decided to lead the NGO initiated by Masterji and grandma, intending to expand its reach throughout India. As Laila set off on her mission, the community came together to bid her farewell at the railway station, showing their support for her noble cause.

xxxx The End xxxx

<u>Synopsis</u>

"Salute the Souls" unravels like an intricately woven fabric of interconnected fates, where every strand contributes to a complex narrative. It brims with the deep-seated emotions of love, selflessness, and courage. The story begins its journey by introducing us to a mother and her son standing before the imposing statue of "Masterji." Little do we know that this statue carries the weight of dreams fulfilled and the birth of educational modernization.

A breathtaking flashback then thrusts us into the past, where Masterji, a compassionate soul, raises an abandoned child in the face of cruel societal prejudice. Tejas, this fortunate foundling, emerges from mysteriousness, and their odyssey shines a piercing light on the tribulations they face in their village. Through undeviating commitment and tireless work, they challenge societal prejudices, proving that love and compassion transcend all boundaries.

The tale evolves, unfurling the outbreak of communal tensions that straddle the boundary between Hindu and Muslim villages, connected by a shared road. Against the backdrop of ongoing religious strife, Masterji and John take center stage, dedicating their lives to bridging the cultural chasm and advocating for peace.

One of our heroes, Tejas, emerges as the beating heart of the portrayal. His voyage to college unearths a deep passion for the Indian military services, setting him on a quest to discover his roots and his mother's identity. It culminates in a high-stakes confrontation with Rita, a formidable media tycoon, digging up layers of intrigue and mystery.

Love blossoms in the unlikeliest of places as Tejas sets forth on a college trip to Darjeeling, meeting Sanam in a twist of fate. Their love story spawns, fraught with doubts, misunderstandings, and a series of gripping events that keep readers yearning for a fairy-tale reunion.

The homecoming of Tejas and Sanam to their respective villages reveals a concealed well of communal tensions, catapulting opposition in their path. Now, whether they unite under the shadow of razor-sharp swords or they surrender to adversity is a head-scratcher worth unraveling.

A tumultuous portion of the narrative is consumed by communal riots ignited by the mysterious disappearance of Tejas and Sanam. Tragedy befalls the village, shaking its residents and sowing the seeds of transformation, as they vow to follow communal harmony.

A unique perspective emerges through John's narrative, peeling back the layers of Masterji's life story. Academic achievements, college days entwined with Rita, dynamics of power, and the peaks and troughs of friendship are laid bare, adding depth and complexity to this layered tale. Masterji and Rita's love story ensues in parallel, marked by complicated emotions, misunderstandings, and a tentative promise of a brighter future, illustrating that love, like life itself, is never simple.

Tejas's arduous journey into the Indian Army, complete with friendships, conflicts, and a mission of utmost importance, sets the stage of personal growth and unfaltering duty to protect the border. His romance with Sanam takes center stage, mirroring the battle of two souls against the societal norms and expectations they must defy.

The fable pivots to the simmering communal tensions of Jammu and Kashmir, offering a glimpse into the complexities of dealing with militants and cross-border terrorism. Laila and Omari's roles in the terrorist organization add more layers of suspense and tension, revealing the intricate web of relationships and conflicts.

The spotlight shifts to JK, who joins a terrorist organization to seek vengeance, rescue Laila, and dismantle the network responsible for the chaos. His recruitment and training in the unforgiving terrorist camp evince his unyielding determination.

As the story hurtles toward its climax, JK's mission takes the stage, untwisting with each pulse-pounding moment. He valiantly rescues Laila and confronts Omari, the nefarious terror kingpin, in a crescendo of action and suspense that leaves readers on the edge of their seats.

The grand finale arrives with JK's promise to his friend, offering closure and a poignant reminder of the cycle of inspiration and national duty. Now, whether he fulfills his commitment and escapes the fireworks of the ammunition is another enigma that must be unriddled. The passing of values and responsibilities to the next generation casts a warm glow on the chronicle's conclusion, echoing the indomitable spirit of humanity and its ability to rise above challenges.

In its entirety, "Salute the Souls" is a masterpiece of storytelling that deftly weaves these diverse narratives and themes into a rich canvas of love, sacrifice, heroism, and personal growth, set against the turbulent backdrop of societal and political complexities.

USKE NAIN SHARABI

(Supplemental Song: from Book "YOUR SMILING FACE)

(*Voice*: Mr. Udit Narayan)

"Hay … to dil ko thaam lo…. hay hay dil ko thaam loooo…"
Uske nain sharabi, uske gaal gulabi
uske nain sharabi, uske gaal gulabi
uske hothon ki baat kare kaun
le gayi le gayi le gayi mere dil ka sara chain
kar gayi kar gayi kar gayi mere dil ko wo bechain
han le gayi le gayi le gayi mere dil ka sara chain
kar gayi kar gayi kar gayi mere dil ko wo bechain

Wo din mein khwab dikhaye, wo night mein dream mein aye
wo din mein khwab dikhaye, wo night mein dream mein aye
haqeeqat ki baat kare kaun
laga gayi han laga gayi mere dil mein aag laga gayi
tarsa gayi tarsa gayi mere dil ko wo tarsa gayi

Uske chaal mein jadoo, dil ko kare bekaboo
uske chaal mein jadoo, dil ko kare bekaboo
uske kamar ki baat kare kaun
lalcha gayi lalcha gayi mere dil ko wo lalcha gayi
kar gayi kar gayi kar gayi mere dil ko diwana kar gayi

Uske nain sharabi, uske gaal gulabi
uske nain sharabi, uske gaal gulabi
uske hothon ki baat kare kaun
le gayi le gayi le gayi mere dil ka sara chain
kar gayi kar gayi kar gayi mere dil ko wo bechain

Wo hai tikhi katili, yahan rut hai rangili
wo hai tikhi katili, yahan rut hai rangili
uske yauvan ki baat kare kaun
kar gayi kar gayi kar gayi mere dil ko ghayal kar gayi
kar gayi kar gayi kar gayi mere dil ko pagal kar gayi

Maine puri duniya dekhi, uski sari saheli dekhi
maine puri duniya dekhi, uski sari saheli dekhi
kisi aur ki baat kare kaun
tarpa gayi tarpa gayi mere dil ko wo tarpa gayi
bha gayi bha gayi bha gayi mere dil ko kuri bha gayi

Uske nain sharabi, uske gaal gulabi
uske nain sharabi, uske gaal gulabi
uske hothon ki baat kare kaun
le gayi le gayi le gayi mere dil ka sara chain
kar gayi kar gayi kar gayi mere dil ko wo bechain
han le gayi le gayi le gayi mere dil ka sara chain
kar gayi kar gayi kar gayi mere dil ko wo bechain…han…